T

By

Ken Malcom

****

Published by:
Flushed Hamster Publications

****

Tales of a Teenage Ninja - Book 1: The Beginning

Special Thanks

A very special thank you to my wife, Zeny, who has put up with my schemes, dreams, and other cockeyed ideas for so long. Without her love and support this book would not have been possible, and I am very, very grateful to her.

Thanks to my adoptive mom and dad, Jacquie and Stan Lundy. You have both had a profound impact on my life, and I am forever grateful. I love you both.

Thanks to Rory, my biggest cheerleader. Your enthusiasm and encouragement helped to fuel the drive and determination to get this book up and running. Thank you for believing in me!

Special Note:

This book is a work of fiction. The names of characters in this book are fictitious, as are the characters themselves. These characters are based solely on the workings of my imagination and any resemblance to any person real or fictional, alive or dead, is pure, total coincidence.

The exception to this is, obviously, the reference to Bruce Lee, who, in my eyes, was the greatest martial artist who has ever lived, at least in my lifetime. You can agree with that or disagree with that, as that is my opinion.

Having said that, know that the references to Bruce Lee in this book are totally fictionalized. Bruce Lee never, as far as I know, trained anyone by the name of Soji. I made that up. Any quote attributed to Mr. Lee was actually spoken by Mr. Lee. You can look it up. That, however, is as far as it goes concerning Bruce Lee.

Chapter I: Choices

"How much money you got, scrotum-face?"

Held aloft by the Neanderthal bully, Connor's feet dangled about six inches off the ground, one hand grasping the front of his shirt, another holding him by the collar. The boy was much bigger and obviously much stronger. Connor knew who he was, knew his story…his name, he was certain, was Zack.

The kid was trouble. This, coupled with his menacing size and reputation, gave Connor all the motivation he needed to stay out of his way. Today, however, in a hurry to get to class Connor decided to take a shortcut.

Bad move.

Apparently this was the ogre's lair, the place where this Cro-Magnon liked to hang out and terrorize those who dared to set foot on the territory he had staked out. Kind of like dogs do after they piss around the yard to mark their turf.

"Hey, re-turd, I asked you a question. How much money you got on you?"

It was not so much a question as it was an ultimatum: give me all your cash or get your lungs pulled out through your nose.

The boy pulled Connor a bit closer to where they were almost touching noses. Connor could smell a combination of cigarettes and Cheetos on his breath. Or maybe it was Doritos. What difference did it make?

This guy had 5' O-clock shadow, for Pete's sake! Is that normal for an 8th grader? Of course this guy probably belonged in the 10th or 11th grade. Connor guessed his brain to be about the size of a T-rex, which was, allegedly, walnut-sized.

Zack's appearance was enough to frighten any middle-school kid, some high-school kids, and, quite possibly, several adults.

He was big, for one. Not fat big, but muscular big. He was tall with broad shoulders. Connor guessed his height at about six feet. Not many middle school kids got to 5-1/2 feet, but then again Zack was not supposed to be in middle school.

Zack had a head of shaggy brown hair which was always an unkempt mess, never brushed or combed. He washed it once, maybe twice per week, but the odor that emanated from his body threw even that generous guestimation into doubt.

Perhaps this was his preferred environment, Connor thought. Zack's master plan was to keep failing until he was either too old to continue in school or until the administration just passed him to get him out of there (this second option was the more likely of the two scenarios).

Here he was the big dog on the porch, towering above the rest of the kids on the yard. Most of the kids in this school hadn't reached puberty yet, whereas this meathead should be dating college chicks, if he were actually smart enough and attractive enough to get the attention of one.

No one would dare challenge Zack. Make all the clichéd comparisons: David vs. Goliath, the 300 Spartans at the battle of Thermopylae, whatever. The point was anyone going head-to-head with this guy faced odds that were just as daunting, though the outcome was never anything to cheer about.

The Spartans lasted three days, brave and defiant to the end, but ultimately lost, fighting to the last man. This was the kind of stuff that you drew on to face certain defeat with dignity, honor, and maybe a little hope that you COULD pull off a stunning victory.

With Zack, however, it always ended the same: strong bully approaches (ambushes, actually) tiny, elf-like middle school kid who proceeds to lose control of his bodily functions, then crumples like a tricycle getting hit by an 18-wheeler. There are no last stands, no stirring words before defeat, no dignity or honor. The end always resulted in some poor sap getting his ass kicked and his money, if he had any, taken by force.

Residual effects were more damaging: the embarrassment of getting your ass handed to you in front of your classmates, then having to walk around school the rest of the day muddied and bloodied, and the feeling of helplessness that always accompanied these assaults.

Zack shook Connor back to reality. “Hey, butt-breath. I’m gonna ask you one…last…time. How much you got?”

By this time a small crowd had gathered. Connor had no illusions about anyone coming to his rescue. People these days didn’t stand up for what was right, and today would be no exception.

In the midst of the crowd Connor was alone, on his own. The strong were allowed to indulge themselves at the expense of the weak while the sheep just let it ride, man, as long as they didn’t have to get involved.

Connor was fairly confident that no matter what he did he was going to get the crap kicked out of him.

Fine…so be it. Was he scared? Yes. However he wasn't going to whimper and cry in front of all these people. He wouldn't give any of them the satisfaction. If they wanted to see blood, they were probably going to get to see blood.

The sheep, however, would not see him cower and beg for mercy. Not today. Screw that. Connor was many things, but he wasn't a sheep.

Connor stared into the eyes of the troglodyte, calm, determined, and steadfast…scared to death, but steadfast nonetheless. He took a long, deep breath before speaking, staring straight into the endless abyss that was Zack's eyes. "You want my money? You're gonna have to take it from me."

Zack looked momentarily bewildered, as if nobody had ever dared talk to him in such a manner. "'Scuze me? I don't think I heard you right, worm."

Connor steeled himself for what was about to come. "Well, maybe your head is too far up your ass to have heard me right. Let me put it in terms even someone with your limited brain capacity could understand: you want my money, you're gonna have to take it from me. I'm not gonna just hand it over. So do whatever you're gonna do, just get it done."

That, it seemed, struck a nerve. Zack's eyes widened, his face turned a couple shades of crimson. Did this little worm just say what he thought he said? Apparently no one had ever challenged him like this, and it took him totally by surprise.

"Someone's getting a whuppin'!" came a cry from the crowd.

"He told you!" said another.

The bully looked annoyingly at the crowd, but only for a moment. He then turned his attention back to matters at hand.

Connor knew he had scored a verbal hit. He started to think about the Spartans standing in the pass, overwhelming odds against them, how brave they were.

Wait…the Spartans all died in the end. Not a good analogy. Stupid Spartans.

Maybe Zack would just drop it and forget the whole thing out of respect for this little turd who was brave enough to challenge his overwhelming superiority. Yeah…right. Brave wasn't the right word…stupid was more apt.

Zack was pissed, that much was evident. He had just been embarrassed in front of a crowd of onlookers. Chum in the water. His hands tightened their grip on Connor's shirt, and now they really were touching nose to nose. Gross.

Connor's heart was pounding. He tried to convince himself that the shaking in his legs was from the cold air surrounding him, except that it was the middle of April, and it was 80 degrees.

At any rate, he had said his piece. Now he just had to wait for the response. He didn't have to wait long.

Chapter II: Dignity

Connor was late to class. A torn shirt, mud-smeared jeans and a split lip told the story of how "Connor's Last Stand" had played out, which was to say not well at all.

He could feel the eyes on him as he strode towards his desk, books in hand. The teacher, Ms. Barber, looked at him as a cat's owner looks when brought a dead bird as a gift.

A couple of the students giggled at his disheveled appearance, but for the most part remained silent. A few of his classmates had been members of the studio audience for the performance that morning.

To Connor's credit he never cried, never complained, never whined. He mustered as much dignity as he could and sat down at his desk, meeting Ms. Barber's gaze over the kid in front of him.

"Mr. Lundy, may I inquire as to what misfortune has befallen you?"

Ms. Barber had a particular manner of speaking: never simple, always proper. Why couldn't she just ask "What happened to you?" or how about "Are you alright?" No, it always had to be "proper" English, whatever that was.

"Mr. Lundy? I am awaiting your answer."

Connor snapped back to reality. "I, uh…I…Well, you see, Ms. Barber…The truth of the matter is, I took a shortcut to school this morning, because I was running late, you see. I was unfamiliar with this shortcut and I slipped and fell on a tree root, which caused me to tear my shirt, and when I fell I hit a patch of mud. So, um, that's why, you know…I mean, that's what happened."

More muffled giggles from the peanut gallery. Connor ignored them.

"Do tell. How did you injure your lip, then?"

"I'm not sure, actually. I think that, um, I must have hit another tree root when I fell, or something. I really wasn't paying attention."

"So I can assume that this is also your excuse for your tardiness, hmmm?"

"Yes, ma'am. Not that it's much of an excuse, really. I mean, I guess I shouldn't've left my house so late, so it's really my fault, I suppose…possibly."

"Indeed, Mr. Lundy. Please see that it does not happen again."

"Yes, ma'am. I apologize for the disruption." Connor was polite to a fault, and he always treated the adults with a modicum of respect. These were virtues his parents had instilled in him long ago.

Ms. Barber considered him for a moment longer. She appeared ready to say something, then thought better of it and turned around to continue the lesson.

Connor could still feel the eyes of his classmates on him, but he didn't care. There were a few of them who witnessed what he had endured this morning and they did nothing. They just watched while Connor got the snot beat out of him and then robbed of his lunch money.

Other classmates who weren't there were no different than those people who just HAD to stare at the car wreck as they passed, hoping to see a body, or at least some blood and guts. Rubberneckers, his dad called them. He could feel the anger begin to well up inside him again. He took a deep breath and let it go.

"Pssst…pssst! Connor, dude!"

Wade, his best friend, was trying to get his attention. Wade sat one seat over and one seat back.

He tried again, whispering loudly. "Dude! What the hell happened to you, man?"

Connor gave him a severe look as if to say "Shut up!" He emphasized this by putting his finger to his lips and jerking his head toward the front of the room.

He had dodged a bullet with Ms. Barber. She was not usually so forgiving of tardiness. Usually the offending student was given detention or made to write some meaningless essay about punctuality or respect.

Perhaps she took pity on him or maybe she just didn't feel like dealing with the drama today. Either way she didn't pursue the issue and he wasn't about to push his luck.

"Dude! Spill, man. Come on! What's up?"

"Shut up!" Connor mouthed silently. He saw Ms. Barber start to turn his way and snapped upright in his chair, eyes forward, just in time for Ms. Barber to miss him. She peered around the class, gave a disapproving look, and turned back to the white board.

Connor looked at Wade and mouthed the word "later." Wade started to say something but Connor cut him off, making a slicing motion with his hand across his neck, the universal sign meaning "stop!" Wade (finally) took the hint.

****

Lunch time found Connor under a tree on the yard, alone. He pondered the morning's happenings, wondering if there were anything he could have done differently. Get up on time, number one, and don't take shortcuts one is not familiar with, number two. Other than that, things worked out as they were going to, he supposed. It's not like he could have taken on Zack and won. Sure he had gotten his ass kicked, but at least it had gotten kicked with dignity! O.K., his lip was swollen, his shirt was ruined, and he was a muddy mess, but that was a small price to pay for his dignity.

"Dude!"

Connor looked up to see his best friend, Wade, trotting his way. Connor really wasn't in the mood to talk, but he couldn't turn his best friend away, could he?

"Dude…'sup?"

"Just hanging out, pondering things, you know?"

"That must have been one nasty tree root to split your lip like that, yeah?"

"Yeah, I suppose. I should learn to pay attention more."

"Horse crap! Tree root my left eye, man. I heard what happened. Are you out of your freakin' mind? What the heck were you thinking, spouting off to Zack like that? You got some kind of death wish?"

"What was I gonna do?" Connor snapped. "I can't beat him, can't whip him, he's bigger and stronger than I am! Let's look at my options:

"One: roll over like a chump and give him my money, then get my ass kicked, or two: keep a shred of dignity and stand up somewhat and then get my ass kicked. Either way, my ass was getting kicked. You know it, I know it. End of story. It's not like someone in the crowd was going to come forward and help me. When your feet are dangling six inches off the ground while being held by the shirt your options are fairly limited, you know?"

Wade turned this over in his head for a moment. They were best friends, sure, but they had much different approaches towards life. Connor was studious, intelligent, polite, a bit uptight and somewhat of a light-weight.

In other words: the perfect target for bully types. Connor also had a very keen sense of right and wrong and was loathe to break rules.

Wade, on the other hand, was more laid back. He wasn't very studious at all, and while he was smart he didn't really take school all that seriously. Wade also had a keen moral compass, but was more willing to bend the rules than his best friend.

"I can see your point, dude. Sorry I wasn't there for you, not that it would have made much difference. At any rate, you got some real brass ones, man. Most people would have just cried and handed over the cash. You stood your ground and took it like a man. Standing up to a certain whupping at the hands of that guy takes guts."

This semi-praise made Connor feel somewhat better. "Thanks, Wade. No sweat."

"No problem. Just stay away from Zack, alright?"

"I'll do my best."

"I know you didn't eat lunch 'cause you got your money stolen, so I brought you a Milky Way. Milky Way is your fave, right? Oh, here's a bottle of water, too."

"Thanks, dude. I'll pay you back."

"Shoot…you don't owe me anything. You earned it today. Besides, it all comes back in the end. Karma-Train and all that. Don't sweat it."

The bell rang, signaling the end of the lunch period. As Connor and Wade trotted back to the building in silence Connor held his head a little higher, almost forgetting about this morning's spectacle. For the moment, anyway.

Chapter III: Rock and a Hard Place

The incident with Zack was but a distant memory for Connor. While he had seen him around the school a few times, he escaped his notice each time. Seeing Zack didn't strike fear in Connor, but neither was Connor going to give the guy the opportunity to give him another pounding.

The day went without incident, other than Connor spilling his books in the hallway as everyone was trying to get to class. It was Friday and Connor just wanted to get the day done and get home. 2:15…almost time. Five more minutes.

The minutes trickled by one after another as they always do towards the end of the school day, doubly so on Fridays. In this last hour of school before the weekend Earth minutes always seemed like Jupiter minutes to Connor.

This was a misnomer, of course. Jupiter actually rotates on its axis once every ten hours as opposed to Earth's 24 hour day. In Connor's mind, however, it just made sense that Jupiter was 1300 times Earth's size, therefore it took longer to spin on its axis, and ergo Jupiter had longer days.

Finally the bell cut loose. While the sound of the bell was certainly annoying to most it brought a feeling of sweet freedom to the students who were held captive by its schedule. Connor was almost the first one out the door, even though he sat towards the back of the class.

"Dude! Wait up!" Wade ran to catch up to his best friend. "What's the rush, man?"

"What do you mean? It's 2:20, the bell rang, end of the day, let's go home."

"Yeah, but you were gone like a shot, dude. You got a date?"

"As if. I'm not exactly date material, you know?"

Wade cut loose with a chuckle. "Don't be so hard on yourself, dude. We've got time."

"True. Not that I'm all that worried about it. You want to go digging tomorrow?" Connor considered himself something of an amateur archaeologist. He had some prime spots along the train tracks by the river where he had found a multitude of fossils, mostly clam shells, but also a few trilobites, some shark teeth, and a prehistoric shrimp. Wade often went with him, fascinated with the things they often found.

"Sure thing. About seven then?"

"Alright. Seven it is."

"I have a spot I want to try, a little further away from the tracks, a little further inland. Not far, maybe a couple hundred yards. I think we may find some interesting stuff."

Connor looked at his friend, genuinely shocked. "Man, you've given this some thought, haven't you?"

"What, I can't have a good idea once in awhile? It just so happens, my good friend, that I really enjoy our little archaeological digs."

"Give me a few years, I'll make an archaeologist out of you yet!"

"Surfing archaeologist? Cool!"

They shared a laugh as they continued home.

****

As they neared their neighborhood they happened upon a group of kids gathered around some sort of commotion. Connor was not the type to gravitate towards crowds.

Wade, on the other hand, liked to stick his nose where it may or may not belong. Being the more adventurous of the two this made sense, however Connor believed that had the potential to lead to trouble more often than not.

"Dude, let's check out the goings-on over there."

"Dude, let's not and say we did. Whatever is happening is not our concern."

"What if someone needs help? What if they've found a wounded duck and it needs help? Come on, ding-dong."

Connor shook his head as he trotted along behind his best friend. "A duck? Really?"

Connor glanced towards the crowd and saw what the cause of the commotion was: Zack. Apparently Zack had increased the size of his territory to include the area just outside of his neighborhood. Great, Connor thought. Just great.

Connor's first inclination was to just keep walking towards home, and safety. He had no desire to get his head pounded in a second time, and this crowd was even bigger than the one that had stood by while he was being mercilessly pounded those few days back.

Yet something in him kept him going towards the crowd, for wherever there was Zack, there was surely someone having a bad day on the receiving end of Zack's own special brand of grade-school terrorism.

"Let's have a look, then…" he said to Wade.

Against his better judgment Connor began walking towards the crowd. He didn't feel in control of his movements. It was as if something, or someone, was directing him to go stick his nose where it may, or may not, have belonged.

He began to press through the crowd trying to get a better view of just what it was Zack was doing to whom, with Wade close behind. He finally got through to the front.

There was Zack, the pea-brain Neanderthal. In front of him, being held fast by Zack, was a boy that Connor did not recognize. The boy in Zack's grip was smaller than Connor. Where he was about 5 feet 4 inches, the boy Zack was terrorizing couldn't have been more than 4 feet 6 inches; almost a full foot shorter. Zack, by contrast, was almost 6 feet tall.

Memories of the day Zack stomped the bejeezus out of him began to flood his mind. His knees began to shake and his heart began to pound in his chest. Fight or flight, his body asked…and his brain said "Flight, stupid, flight!" Connor's feet stayed put, though.

Wade leaned towards his best friend. "Dude, not cool at all. Zack is gonna pound that little pipsqueak for sure."

"What?"

"That kid doesn't stand a chance, man! Look at him! I mean, Zack has a full two feet on that guy."

"Do you know the kid?"

"Nah, never seen him before. He looks Chinese, or Hawaiian, or something. He is one tiny dude, dude."

Then it struck Connor: here he was, in the "studio audience," as he thought of it. He knew that nobody was going to help that kid…no one would stand up to Zack, the bad-ass grade school terrorist who should be in high school…or better yet, Connor thought, prison. Here he was, watching from the outside, just as his classmates had done when he was getting his clock cleaned by Zack.

The anger and embarrassment he felt on the day Zack beat him to a pulp and stole his money began to fester in his mind. He glanced at his buddy. Wade saw it in his eyes but by the time he had processed what was happening it was too late: Connor was walking into the fray.

****

Connor stepped out of the crowd, hesitantly at first, then with a little more confidence, and walked over to where the small boy was standing. He looked him over briefly, and then turned his attention to Zack, who seemed a bit amused at this latest development.

Connor was scared to death, but he couldn't just stand by and let this kid get a beatdown from this punk. That wouldn't have been right, and he wouldn't be able to look at himself in the mirror had he left this kid to get pummeled.

Yes, he was going to get pummeled instead, and he knew that. What the hell was he doing here, again? He reminded himself to smack Wade if he made it out of this mess alive for not doing more to restrain him.

Zack fixed his gaze on Connor. "What the hell do you think you're doing, Twinkie? Get out of the way before I wipe the ground with your face."

Connor stared at Zack with cold eyes, forcing himself not to turn away, even though his brain was screaming "RUN!!!" inside his head. He sized up the situation, took a deep breath, and spoke.

"I don't think so. You want to pick on someone, pick on someone closer to your own size." His legs were really shaking now. He could scarcely breathe, let alone talk.

He thought he might actually try to fight back this time. Maybe he could land a punch or two, as ineffective as they might be. "Leave the kid alone."

Wade ran over to Connor, incredulous at the sheer *stupidity* of his friend.

"Dude, what are you doing? Leave the brute to his business. Let's just turn around, and let it be." He tried to steer Connor away from the fight but Connor planted his feet and stayed put.

Zack looked over to Wade, then back to Connor. "Listen to your little boyfriend, twerp. You're going to get killed. This doesn't concern you, so back off and I *might* forget I saw you. Emphasis on the *might*."

Connor cut a sharp look to Wade, then back to Zack, then back to Wade again. "Wade, unless you're here to back me up, then please, *back…off.*" Connor spoke quietly, but firmly. He emphasized the last two words with force.

Now this took Wade by surprise. He and Connor had never spoken to each other in any other manner than as best friends. Connor, however, had anger in his eyes, and it actually freaked Wade out a bit.

But this was his best friend, and his best friend was about to get pounded…badly. He was beginning to believe his best friend was trying to make this a habit. But as his best friend, was he not obligated to stand up to danger with his friend? Or was he just obligated to advise his friend of how stupid his actions were and just how they would be a detriment to his overall well-being? This wasn't his fight! "But it is your best friend…" his conscience kept telling him.

Wade resigned himself to his position and muttered silently to himself. He could not abandon his best friend. That would just be wrong on so many levels.

"I'm here for ya', dude…*even though you're a frickin' lunatic!"*

Connor sized up his friend for a moment, then turned his attention back to Zack and the kid, who could have been Chinese or Hawaiian…he wasn't sure. He put on the best Clint Eastwood face he could muster, not doing a very good job of it.

"I told you: you want to pick on someone, pick on someone closer to your own size."

The line was crossed; the gauntlet tossed. There was no escape now, and a beating was inevitable at this point.

"Yeah…" Wade chimed in. "You want to pick on this kid, you go through us first!" Wade almost choked on the last words, trying to sound like he meant business. It almost sounded good. Connor just kept staring at Zack, the anger welling up more with each passing minute.

Zack grinned, dropped the kid, and turned towards the duo, both of whom were obviously not quite right in the head…

"Alright, then. Your funeral."

Zack prepared to go to work.

****

Zack pushed the boy towards Connor and Wade. The boy stumbled, almost falling into Connor, who grabbed him and guided him towards Wade. Connor then stepped in front of him, putting himself squarely in Zack's line of fire.

Connor squared himself, bracing for the brutal beating he was about to receive. He was startled when the kid began poking him in the side. "Excuse me?"

Connor turned towards the boy with some irritation. "What?"

"I said: excuse me."

"Excuse you, what?"

"You really don't need to do this. I'm good, really."

Zack hesitated as he strained to hear the conversation over the noise of the surrounding crowd.

Connor looked at the kid with a mix of frustration and amusement. "You're good. Really. Do you happen to have any idea what's about to happen? You're about to get your face punched in. Well, actually now Wade and I are going to get both our faces punched in. So, just chill out and let us handle this."

Neither Wade nor Connor had any illusions about the fact that Zack could take them both on, beat them like drums, and never break a sweat.

The kid piped up again. "No, really…you don't have to do this. Please, just step back and stay out of the way."

Connor didn't know if the kid was just delusional or so scared he couldn't think straight. Either way he wasn't going to leave him here to face Zack alone.

"Did Zack already punch you in the head? Are you nuts? Just pipe down, alright? I've dealt with this guy before."

Zack was getting angrier by the second. "I'm tired of dicking around with you two. You're all going to wish you'd never been born when I get done with you!"

Just as he was walking over to grab Connor a voice yelled from across the street. "Hey! What are you kids doing?"

The crowd turned as one to see where the voice had come from. It was Mr. Finn, one of the teachers from school who lived in the neighborhood. He was driving by and stopped when he saw the crowd of kids standing in a circle, the universal sign of trouble brewing as understood by adults and, especially, school teachers.

"Get home, all of you, and quit loitering around here!"

The crowd began to disperse, quickly. Connor, Wade, Zack, and the kid who may have been Chinese or Hawaiian (they weren't really sure which) began to leave as well but were stopped by the Mr. Finn.

"Not you…" he said motioning to the four boys. "Which of you boys would like to fill me in on what is going on here?"

Zack put on his cheerful face. "Nothing, Mr. Fink…I mean, Finn. Nothing at all. We were just, uh, comparing notes from class today. Isn't that right?"

Connor began to say something but Mr. Finn cut him off. "Comparing notes…right. I know you…Zack, isn't it? Yeah, I know you, alright. If you're in the center of a crowd I'm sure nothing good will come of it."

He turned towards the trio. "Are you boys alright?"

"We're fine, Mr. Finn. Thanks."

The relief Wade's voice was evident. Connor, however, still had his eyes locked on Zack, arms across his chest, face set in stone.

This disquieted Zack, but just momentarily. Zack was used to being obeyed, people cowering at his mere presence. The look on Connor's face was pure hate with anger on the side, garnished with venom. Zack was not used to having his authority challenged.

"Zack, scram." He jerked a thumb towards the road. "You boys come with me."

As Zack began to walk off he kept his gaze fixed on Connor. He didn't say anything. He didn't have to. He just stared and smiled that smile that said "I'll be seeing you…," and not in a good way.

Wade was immediately relieved to see Mr. Finn walking up. Beat down averted.

Connor, however, had mixed emotions. He felt some relief, to be sure, but at the same time he was somewhat disappointed. How dumb was *that*? Maybe he *did* have a death wish.

Connor knew he was going to be in for a rough time. This wouldn't be the last time he would tangle with the school terrorist. Zack would surely be hunting him down to finish what had been started then most rudely interrupted. It was at this point he began to wonder if he hadn't stepped in a deeper pile of poop than he could handle.

In addition, Wade was now involved and was surely going to be on Zack's mind as well. At this point, however, he didn't care about any of this. Wade made his choice. His conscience was clean, and he would deal with the consequences of his actions when necessary.

****

As it turned out the new kid, who may or may not have been Chinese or Hawaiian, lived on the same street as Connor and Wade. Mr. Finn dropped all three boys in front of Connor's house.

"You boys need to be careful. That boy is not someone to mess with. He is dangerous and won't think twice about beating you with no mercy. You're lucky I happened by when I did. You understand me?"

"Yes, sir," they all said in unison.

"Now all of you get home and stay out of trouble."

"Yes, sir," they all said in unison again.

He jumped into his car, cranked it up and put it in gear. They watched in silence as Mr. Finn drove off, a light haze of whitish exhaust trailing from the tailpipe of his '77 Volvo.

The three of them stood in silence for about a half-minute. Connor was about to say something when Wade smacked him in the back of the head.

"Ow! What'd ya go and do that for?"

"Dude! Are you nuts? Have you lost all control of that pea-brain of yours? Tempting fate once, you got away with it. Now you go and do it again! What's gotten into you, man?"

"Look at this kid, man! He is less than half Zack's size! Can you honestly stand there and tell me you would just let Zack bash his head in?" Connor stood there wide-eyed and red-faced.

"As a matter of fact," Wade began, "…I could have, yes, absolutely! I don't know this guy, but I sure as heck know Zack!"

"I can't believe you! Imagine if that was you in his position, crowd egging on a fight and you're facing the beating of your life over…what? Some tough guy decides he has to prove he's the big dog on the porch by beating your ass while a crowd watches, like live theater or something!"

"Why should I stick my neck out? Better him than me!"

"Hey! No one told you to step out there with me! I didn't ask you to come to my rescue! You could have walked away, or stayed and watched, whatever!

"Besides, who was the one who wanted to see what was going on in the first place? Not me! I wanted to keep on going, but noooo! Not you! You just had to see what all the fuss was about! I would have been perfectly happy continuing home but I followed you!"

Connor had him there.

He continued: “Everyone in that crowd was thinking something today. Some were saying better him than me. Some were looking to see some blood. A relative few, maybe one or two, were actually thinking they wish they could do something but they were scared to do so.

"Well, dang it, I was scared but I wasn’t about to let this kid get the crap beat out of him because one delinquent moron has decided that we are nothing more than sheep to be sheared! I’ve lived it! I’ve experienced it! I’ve looked Zack in the eyes while he held me by the neck, and it sucks!”

There was anger in Connor’s eyes, and he could again feel the hatred burrowing up from his innards, creeping into his mind, beginning to control his thoughts and moves. He hated that feeling.

The new kid, who could have been Chinese or Hawaiian, looked on with a mixture of bemusement and curiosity as these two, who were supposed to be friends, went at it. It was a new experience for him, actually.

“What’s the big deal, dude? Why are you so determined to get yourself beaten to a pulp? It’s like you’re on some crusade to rid the world of evil or die trying!”

“You really don’t get it, do you Wade? You don’t have a clue!”

“No, I don’t get it, dude! What’s to get, other than we were this close to getting our heads pounded into our necks?!?” Wade held his index and middle fingers a dime’s width apart to make his point.

Connor stopped for a moment, his mouth hanging open, hand in the air, finger raised as he prepared to make a point. The anger had control of him, and he knew it. It felt good, the rage did, and he knew that was not good at all.

Connor took a deep breath, unclenched the hand by his side (which he had just realized was clenched), and forced the anger back down. He was on the edge of pure fury and knew it. He hadn't felt like this since the first time he had tangled with Zack. This time, however, the feelings and emotions were stronger than ever, and it scared him, quite honestly.

What scared him even more was the fact that he actually liked the feeling of anger. It was a bad emotion, he knew, but was it not serving a purpose?

Wade seemed to sense a shift in the atmosphere as well. He was a bit uneasy as he had never seen his friend this worked up over anything. Really, what was the big deal?

Connor stood up straight, took a look at the new kid (what was his name, anyway?), and then locked eyes with his best friend. He measured his words in his mind before speaking.

"Look, Wade. Let me explain something to you. You remember when I got cornered by Zack that day, and he cleaned my clock, yeah?"

"Yeah, what do you think I've…."

"Shush!" Connor barked as he held a hand up to Wade's face.

Wade was taken aback, but he shushed. "What has gotten into my best friend…?" he thought.

Connor continued: "I have never been one to seek out trouble, and you know that. I have no more desire to get clobbered on a regular basis than you have any desire to play in traffic, O.K.? But, man, what Zack did to me was more than beat me up and take my money…he took away my freedom. Physically he only took my freedom for a few minutes. That was bad enough. But mentally, you have no idea what that does to you.

"You start to live in fear, wondering when it's gonna happen again. You start to alter your way of life in so many ways. You don't take the same path to school, you avoid certain places in the neighborhood, you don't go to certain places to hang out. You are constantly looking over your shoulder or fifty feet ahead to make sure he's not after you again. It sucks!"

Wade had calmed down considerably, not a hard thing for a surfer-type to do. He wanted to say something but Connor continued, cutting him off.

"This piece of *crap* gets to walk around with impunity, terrorizing those he thinks are easy marks, stealing our money, embarrassing us…I'm not going to live like that, dude. And today, I don't know…I saw him getting ready to pound this kid, and I just kind of lost it, I guess. I mean, the brain disconnected from the mind, you know what I mean? I didn't think it through, I just knew I was pissed off and wanted to do something."

Wade pondered this for a moment. "Well, you've done something, all right. You've probably sealed our doom. I mean…well, heck, I'm not blaming you for my involvement. You're right. That was my choice. Nobody's fault but mine. If you hadn't stuck your neck out for this kid I know I wouldn't have. I would have kept on walking, or at the very least watched from the crowd. And I guess, yeah, I did poke my nose where I shouldn't have."

The kid was still standing there, silent, just watching the two friends hash it out.

"I guess what I'm saying is, I'm proud to be your friend, dude. You've got more guts than anyone I know. And you're right. Sorry for giving you a hard time."

Connor smiled a bit. "It's alright. Thanks for not running, even if it meant getting your skull caved in by Zack."

"Hey! You're my best friend, dude! What else could I do?"

"You could have brought me a bat or something…"

At this they both busted out laughing, temporarily forgetting their one-person audience, who looked on in wonder at these two friends who were, apparently, willing to die for each other. Or at least get their heads kicked in for each other.

Chapter IV: Greetings and Handshakes

After the laughter died down, the three of them stood there momentarily in awkward silence, the boy looking at Connor and Wade, who both looked back at him with equal amounts of discomfort and awkwardness. Wade was the first to break the impasse, as he was the more gregarious of the duo.

"Uh…hi. My name's Wade."

"I am pleased to meet you, Wade."

Wade offered his hand, which the boy gladly accepted.

Connor hesitated, then spat out "Connor…my name's Connor."

"I am pleased to meet you, Connor."

Connor extended his hand as well. The boy accepted, and they shook.

Wade turned to Connor, extended his hand, and said "Doctor."

Connor took his hand and replied "Doctor."

"Doctor?"

"Doctor!"

Wade turned to the boy, extended his hand, and said "Doctor?"

The boy took Wade's hand with some trepidation, not sure what was going on but not wanting to offend his new acquaintances. He didn't know what to say so he just kept shaking Wade's hand. "Who is this Doctor fellow?"

"Sorry, inside joke…" Wade and Connor both broke out in laughter again.

The boy, who may have been Chinese or Hawaiian, let slip a wide grin and chuckled a little himself. "I'm sorry. I'm afraid I don't get it." These guys are nuts, he thought to himself.

As the laughter died down again Connor turned to the cause of this afternoon's activities. "…and you are?"

"I am…what?"

"Your name, dude. What is your name? I'm Connor, this is Wade, and your name is…what?" He tried not to sound like a douche, but wasn't too successful.

The boy looked embarrassed. "I apologize. My name is Okita Soji."

Wade attempted it first. "Oki…okita soul food?"

Then Connor. "No, doofus. It's Okita Soshi. Take the wax out of your ears, man. You'll have to excuse my surfer friend. The sun has apparently bleached his brain as well as his hair. He has no culture whatsoever."

Okita rolled his eyes and took a deep breath. "Neither one of you has 'culture,' I am afraid. Let me help you. It is Oh-kee-tah So-gee. No worries, though. My friends call me Nick." He said all of this with a smile, of course. "Thank you for coming to my aid. I am most appreciative to both of you, though it was not necessary."

"Of course it was necessary," Connor said. "You're new around here, yes?"

"Yes. This was my first day at the school."

"Well, a word of advice, short stuff. The guy that was getting ready to use your face for a rake? That'd be Zack, the school thug. He is a tiny warped mind wrapped in an anal cavity. He is a tough dude."

Now it was Nick's turn to look befuddled. "So what is the point?"

Now Nick was not exactly what you would call an athletic looking person. Maybe a runner, but not a linebacker. Heck, not even a punter. He was small, both short and thin. Some would say lanky. Either way he was about ½ Zack's size and Connor and Wade could not understand how this kid just didn't get it.

Wade stooped down a bit to get eye-to-eye with Nick. "The point is, little dude, keep out of Zack's way, 'kay? He is trouble personified, and he'll wipe the floor with you, take your money and anything else he likes, and then kick your dog if you happen to have one. And he'll do it with a Coke and a smile."

"Yeah," said Connor. "Zack is a big, strong guy who will crush you like a soda can if given the chance. You are a skinny stick-boy who will blow away in a strong breeze. Zack would snap you like a twig. No offense, of course."

"Oh, none taken, of course."

"So if you know what's good for you, you will most definitely keep as much distance as possible between you and Mighty Stinky Sphincter as possible, else you find yourself on the receiving end of an unwanted facial rearrangement."

"I see," said Nick, somewhat bemusedly. "Well, I shall remember that. Heaven knows I would not want to have my face remade into something I do not wish it to be."

"Uh…yeah. Couldn't have said it better myself, little dude." Wade was a little flummoxed by this kid. Didn't he understand the grave danger he had been in?

He acted like it was nothing, no big deal. Just another day at the beach, right?

Connor was just as incredulous. Nick was a hair's breadth from getting his clock cleaned by Zack and he just laughs it off? Was this kid off his meds or something?

Connor nudged Wade. "Well, I gotta get home. Late enough as it is."

"Me too," Wade said. "I'll call you later. Or Facebook you, or something."

"Whatever works." Connor turned to Nick. "You live around here?"

"Just down the street."

"Right, you must have been the family we saw moving in last week."

"The same, apparently."

"Alright, then. We'll see you around. Stay out of trouble."

"I will. Please, do not worry about me. I will be fine." He said this with a smile, of course. Connor and Wade, however, got the distinct impression that Nick was just humoring them. It almost seemed like he was patronizing them.

As dusk approached, street lamps began to flicker to life one by one as the three boys headed to their respective homes.

Chapter V: Fossil Hunting

Wade was on Connor's doorstep at seven o'clock sharp the next morning, ready to roll. He was banging on the door for the third time when Mr. Lundy opened the door, clad in his PJs and slippers, substantial hair growth on his pillow-creased face, and bleary-eyed from having just been woken from a sound slumber.

Mr. Lundy was an ultimately cool dad. While he was strict he was fair, and he was always there for Connor, and Wade, whenever needed. Wade thought of him as his adoptive dad even though he had a cool dad of his own. Wade had never seen him angry or upset, and if he had time he would indulge in a little play time with the boys. He had even been on fossil hunting excursions with them two or three times. How many dads did that?

"Wade, are you aware it is seven a.m. on Saturday morning?" Having just woken up, Mr. Lundy's voice sounded bullfrog-like.

"Yes, sir, Mr. Lundy, sir." Wade said this with much enthusiasm. Wade was usually enthusiastic and chipper, no matter the time of day.

"Do you know what people who work for a living like to do on weekends, Wade?"

"Uh, I dunno, Mr. Lundy."

"We like to sleep late. You know, since we're waking up at ungodly hours all week long, and when the weekend comes, we don't have to wake up at ungodly hours, we like to sleep in."

"Huh! No sir, I never made the connection."

"You are WAY to cheerful for this time of morning, especially on a weekend."

"Sorry for waking you, Mr. Lundy. Connor and I are heading out to go fossil hunting this fine morning. He told me to be here at seven. Is he awake?"

"I don't know, honestly. Come on in. He's probably upstairs in his room."

"Thanks, Mr. Lundy!"

"Mi casa, su casa, Wade," Mr. Lundy said unenthusiastically as he turned to go back to bed. Wade made his way up the steps to Connor's room, closing the door behind him.

The door to Connor's room was open a hair. Wade stopped at the door momentarily. Not hearing any movement from inside he pushed the door open gently (thank goodness the hinges didn't squeak!), gingerly making his way over to where Connor lay, still sleeping.

He stood over his friend momentarily, waiting to see if any response was forthcoming. Apparently not. Wade brought his arms up, ready to smack Connor into reality.

"Do it and you're dead," Connor muffled through his pillow.

"Dude! You got eyes in the back of your head or what?"

"No, I could smell you a mile away. You have the odor of a tauntaun carcass left out to rot." He was referring to the creatures that were used on the ice-planet Hoth in the second Star-Wars movie, "The Empire Strikes Back." Wade and Connor were both big fans, even if the Star Wars movie franchise was thirty years old.

"Fun-ny. You're a regular comedian." Wade smacked him in the head. "Get up, dude! The day is wasting away! You're supposed to be up already!"

"Alright, alright! I'm gettin'. Get out so I can get dressed."

"Color me gone, man. Last thing I need is to see you in your tighty-whiteys. I'll be downstairs."

"Be right there. And I wear boxers, by the way."

"T.M.I. dude." Wade shut the door as he left the room and headed downstairs to the kitchen, where he helped himself to a glass of O.J. from the fridge and a banana from the basket on the table.

A few minutes later Connor came bounding down the stairs and made his way to the kitchen as well. "Alright, surfer dude. We need to bring sustenance. You think, what, four bottles of water, a few cereal bars and a couple of apples? That should do for the morning, yeah?"

"Oh, yeah. That's plenty."

"Sweeeet. Let's head out."

"Right behind you, dude."

Connor and Wade went out via the laundry room to the back door. The morning was somewhat chilly, but not unbearably. It would warm up nicely soon enough. A sprinkling of morning dew had settled on the ground and the sun was beginning its ascent. It was a great day for fossil hunting.

****

"Sorry I didn't get a chance to call you last night," Connor said. "Mom and dad wanted to go out to eat and we got back somewhat late. I just went straight to bed."

"Ah, that's alright. I was practicing my finger placement anyway."

Wade fancied himself a guitarist and any spare time he could find he spent practicing. He was actually becoming quite good at it, but still needed a lot of practice. His ultimate dream was to put a band together, like many kids his age.

He wanted Connor to be a part of it, but Connor didn't play any instruments, didn't sing (he couldn't carry a tune in a bucket if his life depended on it), and quite honestly had little interest in music, let alone joining a band. He wasn't sure what he wanted to do with his life just yet but figured he had plenty of time to work it out. After all, he was only thirteen.

To get to the dig location they had to get to the train tracks first, hang a right and follow the tracks to the river. Nobody else knew about their spot for fossils. Actually nobody else was interested, as most of their friends and classmates preferred to stay inside playing games on their PS3s or their Wiis.

Connor and Wade liked video games as much as the next kid, but they had a lot more adventurousness in their blood and preferred to be outside in the elements. Fossil hunting, surfing, playing ball; these were the things that made these best friends tick.

"Anyway," Connor continued, "…what do you think of that kid, Ashy-wasa whatever his name is?"

"Nick, dude."

"Oh, yeah. Nick. I think that guy is off his meds. Is he nuts?"

"Yeah. He did seem a little quirky. Who goes up against someone like Zack and says 'I'm good...No worries...I got it covered.'"

"Tell me 'bout it! He was getting ready to get crushed..."

"So were we, remember, Captain Get Involved?"

"Well, maybe we could have taken him together."

"Who, you and me?" Wade sounded incredulous at the suggestion. "Dude, I'm a surfer, not a fighter. These hands were made for waxin' boards and wailin' on strings, not pounding faces."

"Yeah, I hear you. I just hate having to kowtow to that jerk, ya' know? I wish there were someone who could stand up to Zack who could actually do something about him."

The beating Zack had gifted him with came to the forefront of his mind and he could feel the anger begin to rise again. Wade saw him begin to turn red. He tapped his friend on the shoulder.

"Dude, you alright?"

"What? Oh...yeah. Sorry. Just was thinking about the day Zack pummeled me, that's all. I'm good." And he *was* good. He took a deep breath and let it go.

"Let it go, man. Karma Train never stops running. He'll get his one day."

"Hope you're right. Anyway, forget about it. It's a good day. I don't wanna spoil it talking about that."

"Agreed."

The friends continued on to their destination talking about the things best friends talk about: school, music, and anything else that came to mind.

Chapter VI: Stalked by a (Tiny) Ninja

They arrived at their destination: a spot along the river by the railroad trestle. Their spot was about 50 yards from the tracks and 50 yards back from the river. Wade had another plan, however.

"Connor, see that spot over there? About 20 yards out?" He pointed to a spot on the other side of the tracks that was much closer to the riverbank, but farther away from the tracks.

"You talkin' about that little clearing? What about it?"

"I'd like to try it, see if we come up with anything. Might be worth it, might not, but I think we should give it a go."

"Suits me fine. Let's do it."

It was warming up nicely now and the jackets they were wearing had come off. They arrived at the new spot, took out their equipment and soon began to dig.

The morning went by quickly as happens when one is doing something one enjoys. There was not much talking but there was a lot of digging.

They worked delicately but with purpose. When one of them would hit upon something the brushes came out and they would painstakingly sweep away the layers of dirt that hid their fossilized treasure.

After awhile they took a break. Connor took out two bottles of water and some cereal bars, handing one of each to his friend. They walked towards the tracks to get out of the tall grass that surrounded them, taking a position about ten feet from the rocks that helped to hold the railway in place.

"Hey, man, that was a great idea, trying the new spot."

Wade shrugged. "Yeah, I suppose. Not making any really big finds, though."

"With time, grasshopper," Connor said in the best imitation of a karate master he knew. "Patience…only when you can take the trilobite from my hand will you be a true fossil master."

He looked at Wade with a stern face, but started to smirk, then giggle, and then they both busted out laughing.

"You're not right, dude."

As they began to settle down Connor stopped suddenly, looking over to his left towards the wood line.

"What? Did you see…"

"Hold on, quiet…"

Connor held his hand up, staring at the wood line with intensity. "I thought I saw something out of the corner of my eye, over there, just inside the tree line." He was whispering.

"Dude, why are you whispering? If something is there it's already seen us. Whispering isn't gonna help."

Despite his comment Wade was whispering as well, though he didn't know why. They were in the wide open, after all.

They both sat in silence for a couple of minutes, staring at the trees waiting for…what?

"Dude, what did you see?"

“I don’t know.” He watched the trees a few more seconds, then turned to Wade. “Maybe it was a raccoon or something, or maybe it was nothing.”

“Or maybe it was a bear.”

“Let’s get back to digging.”

“Sure thing.”

While they did not make any colossal finds they did come up with a few items, mainly large bivalve shells and shark teeth like they had found on previous digs. However they also found some gastropod fossils which neither had ever seen before. They were quite pleased with the results of their archaeological expedition. It appeared that Wade’s suggestion had borne fruit after all.

As the sun reached its apex Connor and Wade began to close up shop. The water was gone as were the fruit and cereal bars, and they had pretty much filled their bag with as many fossils as they cared to take home. They would come back. It wasn’t like the fossils were going anywhere.

****

The two were walking down the tracks towards home, their bag full of fossilized shells and sharks’ teeth. They took turns carrying the bag as it was heavy, weighing about thirty pounds. It was quite the haul, they thought.

The day warmed quite nicely. Wade was thinking they should have brought one more bottle of water for each of them for the trip back. Oh, well. Twenty-twenty hindsight.

"When we get back we can grab some lunch at my house and then we'll begin to clean these things up a bit."

"Yeah, dude. That would be copasetic. What's cookin' in the kitchen?"

Wade was getting hungry now. Talking about food always made him hungry. You would never know it by looking at him but he could put away some groceries. Wade wasn't exactly skinny but he could definitely hang a few pounds on that surfer-boy frame of his.

"I don't know. Maybe mom will cook us up something quick if we ask nicely."

"Yeah, your mom can cook, dude."

"What do you…?" Connor stopped as his head snapped to the right. He motioned for Wade to stop as well. He was looking towards the tree line again.

"What now, dude?"

"I could swear I just saw something again. Not in the tree line, but moving through the weeds. Between us and the woods."

"Dude, you are seriously freakin' me out, 'kay? Your imagination is getting the best of you, methinks."

"Thanks. I'll keep that in mind as they cart me off to the asylum." Connor looked annoyed.

Wade and Connor both surveyed the area a few more minutes.

"Well, there's nothing moving there now."

Wade was getting a little freaked out by his friend's behavior. What if he had seen something? What if there was a bear, or a cougar, or something? Wait…did those things even live around here? He made a mental note to do a web search on animals native to the area when he got home this evening.

"Let's just keep walking…quickly." Connor gave Wade a slight push and began to walk with a hastened step. Not that he was worried, but why take chances? Besides, they were almost back to the main road. Once they got to the main road there were houses, and where there were houses there were people, and where there were people there was relative safety…usually.

****

It took about seven minutes to reach the main road. Connor continually scanned their surroundings, keeping watch in case whatever it was he (thought) he had seen decided to return. Nothing materialized, however.

Once they reached the main road they slowed their pace somewhat. The rest of the walk home was uneventful, allowing Connor to relax a little. Another fifteen minutes and they were at Connor's house.

Mrs. Lundy made spaghetti for the boys, complemented with garlic bread and sweet tea to wash it down. (Connor's mom made THE best spaghetti, hands down, in Wade's mind.) Mr. Lundy joined them for lunch as they discussed their archaeological dig while Mrs. Lundy left to run errands.

You could tell Mr. Lundy was definitely Connor's dad. They had the same build, though Mr. Lundy was significantly taller. They both had brown hair. Where Connor's hair was thick Mr. Lundy was balding front to back. A few more years and he would be Friar Lundy, not that Wade would ever tell him that of course.

If you had to guess you would think that Mr. Lundy was an accountant, or maybe a school teacher. He just had that look. He was still one of the coolest dad's, though.

After lunch Mr. Lundy went back to doing whatever it is dads do on Saturday afternoons while the boys went out back to begin cleaning their haul. It was a fairly meticulous process involving a modicum of delicacy.

They had researched how fossils were supposed to be handled and though the things they had found were fairly sturdy they weren't taking any chances. They handled each piece as if each one would shatter with the slightest touch.

The two had been cleaning awhile when Nick happened by. Connor saw him first and called to him.

"Hey, Nick!"

Nick looked over and gave a wave. Connor and Wade both motioned for him to come over, so he did.

As Nick walked up the driveway Wade stood up. "What's up, little dude? Staying out of trouble?"

Nick, with that ever present smile and his hands in his pockets, shrugged his shoulders. "Of course. Why would I go looking for trouble?"

"Well, trouble seemed to be looking for you yesterday, and it found you, no doubt about that."

"I avoid it whenever possible. That is the first time I have ever been threatened like that. I don't know what caused that guy to want to bother me. I did nothing to him."

Connor stopped his cleaning and looked up at Nick. "You don't have to do anything to him. He doesn't need a reason to punch you in the head. He just does it. So, again, it would be best if you just kept a lot of distance between you and him. You're tiny, he's huge, that's all the reason he needs to mess with you."

"I shall do my best to avoid him." Nick glanced at the pile of fossils. "What are you doing?"

Wade's face brightened considerably. "Dude! We're cleaning the fossils we found this morning."

"Fossils? What kind?"

"Mostly clam shells and sharks' teeth," Connor said.

"Oh, did you find them down by the river?"

Connor froze, staring at Nick. "How did you know that?" he asked suspiciously.

Oops.

Nick, caught off guard momentarily, searched for an explanation. He came upon one quickly. "I just figured that would be where you would find fossils of that kind. Clams and sharks are water creatures, you found sharks' teeth and clam shells. We are close to the river. It only makes sense."

Wade was unsure what to say, if anything.

Connor looked at Nick a few seconds more, and just nodded his head, satisfied with the explanation. "Yeah, I suppose. I guess it isn't that hard to figure out, yeah?"

"Yeah, I suppose. May I join you and assist in cleaning?"

"Sure, little dude! Have a sit!"

The three of them spent the rest of the afternoon cleaning fossils and getting better acquainted.

Chapter VII: One Good Turn...

School had let out ten minutes ago but Connor had stayed late to talk with Ms. Flores, his algebra teacher. He was having trouble grasping slope and y-intercept. The concept was not that difficult to grasp, but the mechanics of it were eluding him.

The halls were deserted as he made his way to his locker to get his books. He cranked out the combination, opened the locker door and proceeded to rummage about.

By teenage standards his locker was actually quite tidy, though the mountain of stuff threatened to bury him in an avalanche of books and paperwork at the slightest inducement.

He mumbled to himself as he ferreted out the books he would need that evening. "O.K…algebra book, check. English book, not. History…history…right, chapter nine questions. History book, check." He carried on like this for another couple of minutes and, satisfied he had all he needed, slammed the locker shut.

"Ahhhh!"

The face startled him, causing him to drop his books. He had been so engrossed in what he was doing he hadn't noticed that Wade had sidled up to his locker and was standing behind the open door.

"Freakin' doofus!" Connor yelled. "Good grief, man, you almost gave me a coronary!"

He mockingly grasped his chest, feigning a heart attack as he imagined people do when they actually have heart attacks.

Wade just stood there and grinned. "It's good for you, to have a scare like that every once in awhile. Keeps you on your toes!"

"Well, a lot of good that's going to do when my heart bursts out of my chest. Geez." They proceeded to pick up the mess as Connor began to chuckle.

"Aw, you're alright. Big wuss."

Connor packed everything into his book bag and they proceeded to head out of the school. "Man, these halls seem so big when they're empty, ya' know?" His voice echoed the length of the corridor.

"Tell me about it, dude."

Once outside they had to shield their faces as their eyes adjusted to the sun which seemed somewhat brighter than usual. They made their way through the courtyard and out to the main road.

"Good gravy, man, I got a lot of homework." Connor slipped his book bag off his left shoulder and threw it up on his right shoulder. It made a slight "whump" sound as it settled on his back.

"Not me, dude. I finished most of my work in class. I got history and that's it."

Wade hated having to homework. In his mind it wasn't homework, it was school work done at home, which made his home an extension of school, and that didn't sit right with him. After all, home is home, where you should be able to go to get away from school. School work was for school time, and that was that.

"Well maybe you'd like to come over and do my homework for me, since you're already done with yours for the most part."

"Dude, if I wanted to do school work at home I wouldn't have finished my homework at school, now would I?"

"Aw, too bad. Mom's making killer pasta again."

"Dude! Not cool! You would deny me the absolute awesomeness that is your mom's pasta? Man, I thought we were best buds!"

"Hey, hey...ten algebra problems and you are at the dinner table, my friend!"

Wade feigned being hurt. "My most awesome friend, you wound me where I am most vulnerable…my stomach."

"Always know the weaknesses of your enemies."

"Touché."

"So, be at my house around six-ish?"

"You know it!"

****

They rounded the corner to the neighborhood, still talking and yukking it up as best friends do. Wade was the first to see him.

"Oh, crap…"

"What?" Connor said, and then he saw him too.

Zack. Just standing, waiting, with that stupid turd-eating grin on his face. Outside of their neighborhood. They didn't have to wonder what he was doing there, or what he was waiting for. They already knew.

"Dude, this is NOT good!" Wade hissed to his partner.

"I know," Connor replied.

"I mean, this is really not good!"

"I know," Connor said again.

"Dude, this is…"

Connor cut him off. "If you say 'This is not good' one more time, I might slug you myself! Stay calm!" Easier said than done, he didn't say.

They slowed their pace somewhat, not wanting to rush the impending doom that awaited them fifty yards away. Connor glanced at Wade, not really taking his eyes off of Stinky Sphincter.

"Look," he said. "There are two of us and one of him. Just keep walking, don't stare at him, and for Pete's sake don't say anything."

"Sure thing. He's just gonna let us walk right on past without messing with us. He just came to get help with his homework. Dude, we're dead, do you get that? D…E…A…D…dead."

Zack took up a position in the center of the sidewalk, challenging them as they closed the distance between them. The grin had turned into more of a maniacal grimace. Zack was here to talk business, and the talking would be done with his fists.

"Stay cool, man. We can handle this."

"Yeah…right."

Wade was getting jittery. "Somehow I don't share your confidence." He took a couple of deep, meditative breaths to calm himself. The fight or flight instinct was kicking in. At the moment flight was winning out, but he knew that was not an option.

For his part, Connor was feeling extremely anxious as well, but not because he was scared. On the contrary, he was pissed. Really pissed. It was bad enough that this dunderhead terrorized them around the school and such. Now he was on their turf, in their neighborhood!

The anger in Connor was coming to a peak, and he did his best to control it. Not hide it or put it away, but control it. He was ready for a fight, even if it meant getting his face kicked in. Zack had gone too far this time, and he was going to let him know it.

Zack was still in the center of the sidewalk. Connor and Wade took up a position about ten feet from him.

"Hello, turds. Did mommy not pick you up at school today?"

"No, why? Did your mommy ask you to run away from home?" Connor was quite proud of that one. He wasn't sure where it came from but it was kinda funny.

Wade didn't think it to be all that funny at the moment. He looked at Connor and would have smacked him upside his head in any other situation. Right now he figured he better save his hits for the lout blocking their path home.

The insult did not seem to phase Zack, however. "You think you're funny, ball-breath? I'll show you funny. I'm gonna whip his ass first," he pointed to Wade, "...and then I'm gonna whip your ass. Then we'll see just how funny you can be when you're a stain on the sidewalk."

Connor was just warming up. "Hey, you know, I'd really like to see things from your point of view but I can't get my head that far up my ass, you simpleton." If he was going to get his ass kicked he figured he may as well make the most of it.

Wade was incredulous. He was certain that every time Connor opened his mouth the beating was going to be that much more severe. There was no stopping him, however, and Wade didn't try.

The grin fell from Zack's face. "You know what? I'm tired of talking. It's time for pounding heads."

Connor and Wade took up defensive stances: feet spread apart, knees bent, and fists clenched. "Bring it on, big guy." Wade reminded himself to smack Connor when they got out of the hospital. If they survived, that is.

Chapter VIII: Disclosure

The three stood in the middle of the street. "You got an awful big mouth, turd." He said it mockingly, not really taking the two of them seriously. "I'm gonna shut it for you." Zack seemed almost serene, as if he couldn't care less about matters at hand. The look on his face was deceptively calm, and then…

Zack seemed to close the distance with one step as he grabbed for Connor's throat. Connor side-stepped him as Wade fell off to the side to avoid getting crushed. They were much smaller than Zack and therefore much more agile. This would not help them for long, however. Connor wasn't running, and Wade wasn't going to leave his buddy to face Zack alone.

"Come on, ya' freakin' moron. What's the matter?" Connor began to taunt him, a move Wade saw as not very smart.

"Dude, think you can lay off the trash-talk somewhat?" Wade said with a hint of irritation.

"Why? We're gonna get creamed either way." He turned back to Zack. "Come ON, you wuss!"

That got Zack's attention. This time he took one step and leapt, catching Connor by the pants. Zack flung him into the street. Connor landed in the middle of the road, scraping the elbow on his right arm. It burned as rock and sand ground into the abrasion.

Connor got right back up, wiped the wound on his pants, ready to tackle Zack. Wade came 'round to his side, but Connor was already running. He yelled as he lunged at Zack, intending to punch him in the head as he leapt, but Zack just put a leg out as he moved to one side, tripping Connor, who landed in the street again, making the abrasions worse.

At this point Wade saw his opening. Zack's back was to him and his attention was focused on Connor at the moment. Wade ran and took a flying leap onto Zack's back, wrapping his left arm around his neck, punching him in the head with his right.

Zack, caught unaware, let out a yell.

"Gahhh! You frickin' ass wipe...!" Zack grabbed the arm around his neck as he attempted to block the other arm from raining blows down upon his head. Unable to pry the arm away, he fell backwards landing on Wade, knocking the wind out of him.

Zack scrambled to get up, quickly getting to his feet. Wade just lay there, trying to catch his breath. He had never had the wind knocked out of him before, and it was a terrifying experience. For a minute he really thought he was dying.

Finally his breathing returned. He clambered to get back to his feet, but Zack was already on top of him.

This time it was Connor's turn. Zack's fist was at the top of its trajectory, ready to smash into Wade's face as Connor made like a kicker going for the extra point on Zack's rear-end.

The pain exploded in the small of Zack's back as Connor's foot said hello to Zack's posterior. The kick was so forceful it launched Zack about a foot off the ground and over Wade's outstretched body. Zack landed face first on the pavement, asphalt and rock shredding the right side of his face.

Wade hastened to get back up and to his friend's side. This fight was escalating into something very nasty and Zack, now having sustained an actual wound, was sure to be even more enraged.

A tiger was a dangerous thing. A wounded tiger, however, was a dangerous, unpredictable thing.

Connor and Wade were breathing heavily, but they were physically fit which was playing to their advantage here. Zack had size and strength, but Connor and Wade had agility and endurance, not to mention a healthy desire to live.

Connor was fighting for something more than just being able to walk away in one piece. He was fighting for the right to live without the fear of having to look over his shoulder constantly. Not just for him, mind you, but for his friends and classmates as well. He was pissed, and if he went down fighting, so be it.

Zack got up, turning to face his adversaries. His face was bright red and twisted with rage. There was a large abrasion on his right cheek, blood trickling down his jaw line to his neck which was wet with sweat and blackened with dirt.

He started walking towards them, pointing. "I am so gonna rip your head off and shit down your neck! You should have never tangled with me, turd!" He was looking directly at Wade.

The two took up defensive positions once more, the best fighting stance they knew how: fists up, knees bent, left foot in front, right foot slightly back. They were as prepared as they could be for the coming onslaught even though neither had ever been involved in a fight.

Suddenly a small figure appeared. He was about 4'6" tall, somewhat slender, and could have been Chinese, or perhaps Hawaiian. "I wouldn't do that if I were you, Zack."

Zack stopped dead in his tracks, turned, and couldn't believe his eyes. Neither could Connor and Wade. It was Nick.

He had appeared out of nowhere. Connor thought that was weird but then they had been concentrating on the fight, hadn't they?

Nick walked up to where Connor and Wade were standing, all the while keeping eye contact with Zack. His normally cheerful demeanor had disappeared. He looked almost…angry. No, angry wasn't the right word. There was no emotion on his face at all it seemed. The look on Nick's face gave Connor the willies.

Connor came to his senses. Come on, he told himself…Nick was just playing brave. It was easy to do now that there were three of them.

"Nick, what are you doing, dude?" Connor said it quietly but matter-of-factly. "Get out of here."

Nick kept his eyes locked on Zack. "It is time someone put Zack in his place. I am here to do that." He said it loud enough for Zack to hear.

Connor could not believe his ears. Neither could Wade. Neither could Zack. Was he serious?

Zack started to smile, then giggle, and in a few seconds he was all-out laughing.

"You…are here…to put ME…in MY place? You and what army?" He laughed a few more seconds and then regained his composure.

He straightened himself up to his full six-foot height, replaced the maniacal smile with a scowl, and stared straight at Nick. "I don't think so, re-turd." He punctuated the ''-turd" as he always did with his favorite insult.

"Hello! Nick?" Connor tapped his misguided friend on the shoulder.

"Yes?" Nick never turned, keeping his gaze fixed in Zack's direction.

"Are you nuts? Get…out…of…here. Now. You are going to get us all killed. You are not helping matters, you are making them worse. Now please, just go while you still got legs…'kay?"

Wade chimed in: "Yeah, dude…you're not helping. Nothing personal, we just don't want to see ya' get your rear kicked."

Nick never took his eyes off of Zack. "Look you two. I really, really appreciate you looking out for me. I appreciate you trying to protect me from the big, bad bully. There is a lesson you both need to learn…right here, right now."

"This isn't exactly the best time for lessons, you know?" Connor was more than a tad irritated.

"The lesson is this: Do not judge the book by its cover. All is not as it seems, and for you to assume that I am incapable of taking care of myself is arrogant and insulting."

This caused Connor and Wade to feel like a couple of jerks. They had never thought that they were insulting their friend; they had just assumed that…

Ah, yeah. That was the rub now, wasn't it? They had assumed.

Connor began to fumble for an apology, even though this really wasn't the time for it. "Hey, look man…I'm sorry if…But I mean, just look at ya'! What were we supposed to…"

Nick cut him off by holding up his hand. "Never mind. Not the right time or place. We have business at hand, yes?"

He stared into Connor's eyes for a moment with that blank, emotionless gaze…and suddenly flashed a huge smile. "Don't worry, my friends…I got this."

He patted their heads, and as quickly as Nick had shown off that grin of his it was gone again, rendering his face emotionless and distant.

That face…something about it just made Connor uneasy. He felt a shiver run down his spine.

Zack could still not wrap his brain around what he was seeing. This…this…pipsqueak was daring to challenge him. And he looked serious! No matter. He would make short work of him and then finish off the other two.

"Hey, rodent…don't think I'm gonna show you any mercy just because you're a runt! You understand me? You're dog meat!"

He glowered at Nick, his face contorted in a twisted mass of anger and evil. "I am so gonna kick your ass, runt!"

Nick slowly stood upright, bringing his 4'6" frame to its full, totally unintimidating height. He faced Zack and stepped out into the middle of the street, eyes fixed on his nemesis.

He did not display any particular stance. As a matter of fact Connor and Wade thought he looked somewhat…relaxed. An odd defensive posture if ever they saw one.

Zack sensed easy pickings; but that was his mistake. He started towards the skinny little kid in the middle of the street with every intention of wiping the asphalt with Nick's face. This was gonna be fun.

And then it was on. Dude.

Chapter IX: The Good, The Bad, and the Very, Very Ugly

Zack began to move towards Nick, who just stood there looking as disinterested a student in class at five minutes before the final bell on a Friday afternoon. "I'm gonna teach you to stay out of other peoples' business, stick-boy."

Nick did not react. He just stood there, motionless, not making a sound, not moving a muscle other than the rising and falling of his chest as he breathed, and even that was barely perceptible.

Zack kept coming. Fifteen feet...twelve feet...ten feet...

"Holy cripes...!" Wade thought. "He's not doing anything! Is he even gonna defend himself?"

Five feet...Zack brought his arm up and reared back with the intention of punching Nick. A funny thing happened on the way to Nick's face, however. Nobody saw it, but it happened.

Zack was on the ground. Not only was he on the ground, he was a full ten feet away from Nick.

Zack did not even have time to yell, let alone react. All he knew is that he was on the ground face first. His face made contact with the pavement, giving Zack a scrape on his left cheek to match the one on his right cheek.

"What the..." Connor did not finish the thought. What just happened? Did anything just happen? He looked at Wade, who was looking at him with his mouth agape.

"Dude! What was that? I mean…I didn't see him move! Did you see him move? 'Cause I sure as beans didn't see him move! Freakin' cripes, dude!"

Connor was just as befuddled as Wade. "I didn't see him move, either. I think Zack just tripped…or something."

He knew that wasn't possible, however. It didn't look like he tripped, and even if he had he would have fallen on Nick or at least fallen close to him. He was almost ten feet away from him, like he had been thrown! One second he was up, ready to pound Nick's head in; the next second he was down!

Nick had turned and was facing Zack, who was now lying on the asphalt. Zack looked crestfallen, as if his favorite ice cream had fallen off its cone, rolled down his shirt and landed in an ant pile.

Zack never saw it coming. He couldn't believe this kid had just thrown him to the ground.

"That is just not possible…" he thought. "Must've tripped…or something," Zack thought to himself.

He got up and looked over where Nick was standing, searching for the object that would have tripped him up. Nothing. The road was clear of anything that may have caused his fall. Except for that little twerp standing there staring at him as if this is how things were meant to be. Zack refused to believe the twerp actually tossed him ten feet, let alone touched him at all.

"You won't be that lucky this time, turd." Zack walked towards Nick with a sense of purpose. "I'm done screwing with you! Hope you like pain…"

He drew his right arm across his body, preparing to backhand Nick across the face. His arm got about one-quarter of the way there when it was stopped cold and found its way jacked up behind his back, his hand almost touching the nape of his neck. At the same time his legs were swept out from under him. He landed on his back, and his arm, causing him to yell in extreme pain.

"OW! You son-of-a-bitch! You broke my arm! Oh, crap, I think it's broke!"

Zack turned over on his left side to free his right arm from behind him. He didn't try to get up, opting to remain on the ground. He cradled his arm, moaning in pain, his face bloodied from his earlier engagement with Connor and Wade. He lay there, writhing in pain, as Nick watched him from about ten feet away.

David had slain Goliath! The Spartans lived to fight another day!

Connor and Wade just stared at Nick, almost forgetting about Zack. They were stunned. The entire engagement between Nick and Zack lasted all of two minutes from start to finish, trash-talk included.

Zack never even touched him. The two of them tangled with Zack for about ten minutes before Nick showed up, and they were struggling to keep from getting their butts kicked with two-on-one.

For a moment Connor thought Zack was going to start crying, which would have been totally cool. He didn't, however. He just laid there, bloodied face, holding his arm, his face showing the pain he was experiencing at the moment.

Nick, convinced that Zack was not getting up any time soon, turned and walked over to where his two friends were standing. "I told you, I got this." He flashed a quick smile and clapped his buddies on their shoulders.

"Come on. We should leave while the animal lay wounded." He jerked a thumb towards Zack, who was now on his knees and staggering to his feet.

The three friends began to walk towards their neighborhood. Connor and Wade stole a glance over their shoulders as they walked.

Zack had made it to his feet and was still cradling his arm. He stared at them with a burning hatred. "We ain't finished yet! You hear me?! This is not finished! I *will* be coming for you, you hear?!"

Nick stopped dead in his tracks, turning to face Zack. "Well let's not leave things unfinished, then."

He glared at Zack with that dead look in his eyes. Zack just stood there, not knowing what to do.

They stared at one another for a moment. Then Nick stuck a foot out and threw his arms up.

"BOO!"

This startled Zack…no, it freaked him out. He stepped back, turned around and walked away. He didn't look back.

Connor, Wade and Nick watched him skulk away silently. He took a right turn into the woods, taking a short-cut to wherever it was he was going. Most likely under a bridge somewhere, where trolls were supposed to live, thought Connor.

Connor and Wade were at a loss for words. No words were needed, really.

The three boys turned and headed for home.

Chapter X: Flabbergasted

Connor and Wade were staring at Nick in utter amazement and total disbelief.

Nick looked nonplussed. “What?”

Wade seemed the most impressed. “Dude…where did you learn to…I mean, what in…Dude!”

Connor finished Wade’s thought. “Yeah…where did you learn that…that…whatever it was you did?”

Nick seemed unfazed by their amazement. “I told you not to judge by appearance. You never know what lies underneath the surface.”

“Dude! Zack is, like, twice your size.” Wade was still digesting what he had witnessed and could still hardly believe what was seen with his own eyes. “I mean, Connor and I together were having a heckuva time with him, and we were probably about to get our butts kicked, but good, dude!”

Connor was equally incredulous at what had just transpired. “I would never have guessed you had that in you, Nick. What was that? Karate? Judo? What?”

Nick looked a little embarrassed. “Look…I don’t usually use this stuff, o.k.? I mean, yeah, it was necessary in this particular situation. But I don’t like showing it off in front of others.

"As a matter of fact, this is the first time I’ve had to use it. You two, and Zack, of course, are the first to know, and I don’t think Zack even saw what I did.”

Connor and Wade exchanged quizzical looks, but they wanted to know more. “O.K. And…?”

They came to Connor's house and stood in the driveway for a minute. "Look, guys. We're almost home, and it's late. I have a lot of homework to do."

"Dude....come on, man! That was awesome stuff! Tell us about it!" Wade seemed excited about their friend's previously unknown skills. "I mean with the…the…tossing, and the…the…whatever else you did. That was totally awesome!"

Connor was about to say something, then stopped as a sudden realization enveloped his mind. It took a moment, but then…

"Wait a minute." Connor was getting red in the face. "You mean to tell me you have this…this…skill, power, whatever, and you've been hiding it from us all this time? You mean I risked getting my ass beat by Zack trying to help you out and you could've taken him out at any time? Dude, what the hell!"

Wade was confused, and then it hit him as well. "Yeah…Connor's right! I risked my neck for you, too, you little twerp! Well, I wouldn't have if ding-dong here hadn't gone all Clint Eastwood on me, ya' know? But still…"

"Yeah. That's bull, Nick. What are you doing, holding out on us like that?" Connor was truly angry. He felt betrayed.

Nick, hand on his chin, surveyed his friends before answering. "Look, guys. Connor, I appreciate what you did for me, what with taking up for me and all that. I mean, I can understand, given my nerdy 'stick-boy' appearance and all.

"However, if you recall, I told you I had it under control, remember? But you insisted, because you didn't think I was able to defend myself. You judged me by my appearance."

"Yeah, but..." But. But what? Nick was right. He had told him to back off, and did Connor listen? No.

"As a matter of fact," Nick continued, "...I told you that I had the situation handled, and you insisted on pushing me aside, playing the hero, coming to the rescue of the poor, pitiful, skinny little Asian kid. Remember that?"

Connor felt his stomach drop. He had not considered that Nick saw it that way. He thought he was helping someone out. What's more, Nick did, in fact, tell him that he had the situation well in hand. Now he just felt like an absolute heel.

What was worse was because of his brashness Wade had felt obliged to help his friend out which put him at risk of getting his rear-end beat as well. Well, he didn't force Wade to jump in, but still, how could he fault him for that? He was his best friend, after all. What did he expect him to do?

"And finally, first lesson of combat: never, ever give away your secrets. You never let anyone know what you are capable of until you need to let them know what you are capable of, like back there with Zack."

"Look," Connor stuttered. "...I didn't mean it that way, and you know it. I mean, how the heck was I supposed to know? It's not like you said 'Back off, I know karate, I can handle this.' I thought I was helping, you know?"

"I know. But you pre-judged me without knowing anything about me. Look, I really appreciate what you did. That took nads, man. Big nads. Both of you. No one has ever stood up for me like that. I'm a target because I am so small. Bullies pick on those of us who they think are weakest, and let's face it; I look pretty weak, yes?"

"Yes," Connor and Wade said in unison.

"Alright, look. It's late, we have to get in. Tomorrow is Friday. After school, we'll meet up and I'll spill. But you've got to promise me something."

"And that is…?"

"Under no circumstances can you tell *anyone* about what you know, alright? I mean not a single person."

"Uh, o.k." Wade was hesitant. "Why?"

"Just promise: not one, single, solitary soul. You tell anyone, I'll deny everything, and I won't tell you anything."

Wade was persistent. "Why all the secrecy? What's the big freakin' deal?"

"I already told you why. First lesson of combat. Forget it…I can see that you are not going to listen." He started to walk off.

"Alright! Alright! We promise!" Wade started to grab him by the shoulder, but the image of Zack landing ten feet from Nick made him rethink that, and he withdrew his arm quickly.

"Yeah, we won't tell anyone. Promise. After all, we're all friends, right?" Connor was big on the loyalty thing. Friends helped each other out, and they didn't dish secrets on each other, ever, unless it was illegal or immoral.

Nick stopped and turned towards his friends. "Yes, we're all friends. You guys are the best friends I've ever had, even in the short time we've known each other. Now, you promise, not a word, right?"

"Right." Connor extended his hand, and Nick took it. Wade finished the pile as they all shook on it.

"Done, then. See you tomorrow after school. Later guys!"

Nick took off down the street at a light jog. His house was two blocks down the street from Connor's and Wade's houses.

They watched him until he got to the next corner. The street lamps were beginning to glow as sunlight began to retreat.

Connor smacked Wade on the back of the head. "Man, I hope I can get in without the folks seeing me. I really don't want to be explainin' this away."

"Dude, they're gonna see it when you eat dinner anyway, ain't they?"

"Yeah, but I look like crap now." He rubbed his hand across the abrasion on his face. "At least I'll have a chance to clean up a little bit. Maybe they won't notice."

"Yeah, and monkeys might fly out of my butt." Wade began to walk towards his house.

"I'll talk at ya' later, Wade. After I finish homework."

"Sure thing, ding-dong!"

With that they both went indoors.

Chapter XI: The Big Meeting

The school day on Friday was uneventful. Connor and Wade took pains to avoid any encounters with Zack, but they never saw him. Maybe he was playing hooky, or maybe he was injured so severely he had to stay home.

Connor was hoping for the latter. Serves the jerk right, he thought. Either way, Zack's absence was a great relief to them both. One less thing to worry about as the day wore on.

The final ten minutes of the school day were always the slowest, even more so on Friday. Today, however, the minutes turned to hours as Connor and Wade anticipated the cranium-rattling sound of the bell to signal the end of another week of school drudgery. They were both excited to meet up with Nick and learn more about the "mystical can of whoop-ass" (Connor's name for it) he had opened up on Zack yesterday.

The class was mostly silent, save for the girls in the back who were trying to keep from being heard as they whispered back and forth, but mostly failing as Connor could pretty much hear everything they said. He wasn't interested in their conversation, though, and just ignored it. Most of the class was either busy working on their assignment while others just stared out the windows longing for the day to be over.

Connor looked over to Wade, who looked just as impatient as Connor felt. He looked up at the clock for what must have been the gazillionth time since class began.

Two minutes.

He stared at the clock trying to make the second hand move faster by sheer will alone. He did this for a full minute, and then started mentally counting down the seconds as they ticked away. Ten…nine…eight…he put his back pack on his shoulder…three…two…one…

Both Connor and Wade shot out of their seats like rockets the moment the bell rang. Wade almost knocked over Lisa Biggs, who sat directly in front of him and had begun sliding out of her chair.

"Hey, watch where you're going, Wade!"

"Sorry Lisa can't talk now gotta go bye!" Wade hurried to the door that led to the hallway, freedom for the weekend, and most importantly the unveiling of the secrets of the "Mystical Can of Whoop-Ass."

"You are such a weenie, Wade!" Lisa huffed. Wade seemed not to hear her, though, as he continued his trek to get out of the classroom.

He and Connor made it to the door about the same time. "Man," Connor looked at his friend as they began to walk. "You about ran over Lisa, didn't you?"

"I didn't mean to. Besides, I said sorry, didn't I?"

"Yeah, I guess so. Listen, we didn't see Zack all day today, right?"

"Yeah. That was a relief. He must be holed up under his bridge nursing his wounds."

"Well think, man. Just because he wasn't in school doesn't mean he isn't waiting for us on the way home, right?"

Wade stopped amidst the bustle of kids hurrying to get out of school. "Yeah, cripes. I hadn't thought of that."

"I figured. Anyways, we need to take an alternate route, where we are much less likely to run into the jerk."

"Yeah, right.

Connor thought about this for a moment. He was eager to get home and meet with Nick, but he wasn't at all eager to come face-to-face with their nemesis again. Not today.

"Yeah, I guess that'll do. It'll be worth it to avoid the troll. Let's roll."

They both reversed course and went out the end of the building opposite from where they usually left to head home. Connor was mildly irritated at having to undertake this course of action. First: it made him feel like he was running from a problem, that problem being Zack. Second: it was going to take longer to get home and, ergo, longer to meet up with Nick.

Still, the alternative was much worse: run into Zack again, which would take up even more time as they engaged in another fight, one in which it was highly unlikely that anyone would come to their aid as had happened last time.

Connor touched the now-scabbed over scrape on his face, a reminder of his encounter with Zack the day before. Deciding that the risk did not outweigh the benefits Connor just sucked it up, and off the two friends went.

****

The journey from school to their neighborhood took about twenty minutes longer than usual, a minor inconvenience compared to the alternative. As they trekked home they shared their thoughts on what Nick may tell them. They kind of figured he was into martial arts, but why would he want to keep that a secret? It's not like nobody knew about karate and judo.

Connor and Wade both had tried karate classes, but that lasted all of two weeks as they got bored with the repetitive exercises that were expected of karate students, especially the menial exercises carried out by white belts, the lowest rung of the karate ladder. Bo-ring!

Finally they arrived at their neighborhood. The two went straight to their respective houses to drop their school things. They both emerged from their houses at the same time and set out for Nick's house.

****

The walk to Nick's house took about three minutes. They resisted the urge to run, not wanting to look like they were excited about the revelation, though in reality they were very anxious to pick Nick's brain.

They bounded up the front steps to Nick's house and Wade rang the door bell. Looking down Connor noticed the shoes lined up outside the door.

The house was well-kept, neat and tidy. The lawn was nicely manicured with yellow lantana on either side of the front steps.

The door opened without warning catching both boys off-guard. Nick's visage peered at them from the other side of the glass door.

"Whassup fellas? Come on in!"

"Hi, Nick." Connor and Wade started in when Nick held up his hand.

"Guys, could you take your shoes off please? We don't wear shoes in the house. It's a respect thing. Japanese tradition, and all that. Thanks."

"Oh, yeah. Sorry." They dutifully removed their footwear, placing it with the other shoes on the porch, and then entered.

They walked through the living room and to the kitchen where Nick's mom was busy making dinner. She looked up and smiled as they walked in. "Hello, boys."

"Hello, Missus…?" Connor stopped short, embarrassed at having forgotten Nick's last name.

"It is Soji. "

"Ah…Missus Soji. Nice to meet you."

"Mom, these are my friends, Connor and Wade."

"It is very nice to meet you both. Nick told me what you did for him when the bully was messing with him on his way home a few weeks back. It is nice that he has found such friends that will stick up for him."

"Ah, it was nothing. He'd do the same for us, I think."

"Hey mom, we're going out back for awhile, o.k.?"

"That's fine. Connor, Wade, would you like to stay for dinner?"

Nick beamed at his friends. "Yeah, stay for dinner, guys."

Wade was first to respond. "Yes, ma'am. Absolutely! Thank you for asking!"

"Well," Connor started, "I'd have to ask my parents, but I'm sure it will be alright. Thank you."

"You are most welcome."

"It smells great. May I ask what you are cooking?" Connor expected it would be some derivative of Asian cuisine, but his only experience with Asian cuisine was eating at the China Wok with his parents on occasion.

"Spaghetti," Mrs. Soji said. "I hope you like Italian."

Wade pumped his fist in the air as he let loose a huge grin. "Yes, ma'am. Love Italian. Thank you again!"

"And you are welcome, again. Dinner will be ready in just a little bit."

"Thanks, mom. Come on, guys. Let's head out back."

And out they went.

Chapter XII: The Reveal

There was a cement slab out back that passed as a porch of sorts where a brand new picnic table sat. The three sat down with Nick on one side, Connor and Wade on the other. After sitting in silence for a moment Nick spoke up.

"So. What's going on, guys?"

Connor and Wade looked crestfallen. "What do you mean, what's going on? Remember yesterday? Meet you here…today…tell us about the 'Big Secret' you made us promise not to tell under pain of death? Remember any of that?" Connor pointed to the scab on his face.

"Yeah," Wade chimed in. "Come on, dude…spill! We've been waiting all day!"

Nick put his hand to his chin and looked up, trying to look thoughtful. "Hmmm…let's see. What were we gonna talk about…?"

"DU-ude! C'mon, man!"

Nick let out a chuckle. "Aww, I'm just playin' with you guys. Where's your sense of humor, *dude*?"

Connor and Wade deflated a little, but began to chuckle as well. "Touché. Good one."

"Alright, then. Again, I need to stress to you that under no circumstances can you tell anyone about anything I am going to tell you, got it?"

"Got it," Connor and Wade said in unison.

Nick took a deep breath. "The only reason I am telling you two is because you are my friends, and I trust you both. Otherwise I would not be telling you anything."

"Uh, O.K." Wade looked bemused. "So why all the secrecy? Not that I'm gonna dish on any of your secrets or anything, I'm just curious, as is Connor. Right, dude?" He jabbed Connor with an elbow.

"Yeah, right." Connor elbowed him back, a little harder.

Nick studied them both for a moment before speaking. "Do you have any idea what I am going to tell you?"

They shifted in their seats. "Not really," Connor said. "We talked about it somewhat on the way home today, and kind of figured that you knew some karate or something."

"That is the right line of thinking, yes. But it is not karate."

"Well then, what is it? Judo? Tai-Kwon-Do?" Connor was somewhat interested in martial arts and had done some research on the various disciplines.

"Do you guys know who Bruce Lee is?"

Wade's eyes lit up. "You mean the movie guy from like the 1970s? Heck, yeah we know who he is! He was the best martial artist of his time! Still is, far as I'm concerned. 'Enter the Dragon' is one of my favorites!"

"Do you know what it was that Bruce Lee practiced? I mean, what school of martial art?"

"I always just thought it was karate. But he made it look so cool!"

"Yeah," Connor joined in. "Bruce Lee is the ultimate in martial-arts."

"Well, Bruce Lee started out by learning a martial art called Wing Chun Kung Fu. He excelled at it, but decided that it needed refining. He came up with the concept of Jeet-Kune-Do."

Connor and Wade had never heard of it. "Jeet-what?" Connor asked.

"Jeet-Kune-Do."

"And he created this, all by himself? A whole new martial art?" They were more than a little intrigued now. Nick had their complete attention.

"Well, that's a little misleading. Jeet-Kune-Do is actually a blend of a few different styles of martial arts. It is mainly a modification of Wing Chun Kung Fu, but also incorporates American-style boxing and, believe it or not, fencing."

Connor was amazed, even if he had never heard of Wing Chun Kung Fu. "Boxing and fencing? What do those have to do with martial arts?"

"Dude, that sounds way awesome." Wade was just as impressed. "So you use swords and stuff? Neat!"

Nick continued with the patience a mentor shows to his disciple. "No, no swords. It is the mechanics and techniques of the art that are incorporated, not the weapons.

" On TV and in the movies you see these guys doing all kinds of kicks and blocks and stuff. That's all Hollywood. I mean, some of the stuff you see is actual martial-arts stuff, but most of it is just for show, you know, to make it look "cool" and all that."

"Go on…" Connor urged.

"Well, that's it, really."

Wade was puzzled. "So why all the secrecy? I mean, I would think you would be lettin' everyone know you're a badass, man."

Nick shook his head slowly.

"No. Not at all. You never want to expose your strengths or weaknesses to anyone. Remember: first rule of combat. If, like me, you have some martial-art skill, there are people who will want to challenge you all the time. They want to be the one to be able to say 'I beat karate boy' or something like that. They're looking to show they're a tough guy, too.

"If potential enemies know your weaknesses then they know how to go after you to defeat you. It doesn't mean they will beat you, but it will make it that much harder for you to finish the fight quickly.

"If potential enemies know your strengths then they know how to prepare for a fight with you. It ruins the element of surprise.

"These are the reasons I asked you to keep this between the three of us. I don't want anyone to know about this."

"Zack knows about it." Connor pointed to the scab on his cheek.

"Well, does he really? What does he know? All he knows is that 'something' happened to him. He may well think he tripped and fell. One thing is sure, he isn't going to go around telling anyone he got his butt beat by some puny guy like me."

Wade stifled a laugh. "Yeah, tell me about it."

Nick chuckled. "Let's face it…I'm not exactly the picture of manliness, am I?"

And with that they all laughed. Connor thought it was cool that Nick was so down to earth even though he could probably whip anyone in the school, and probably anyone in the high school. What's more, he could laugh at himself which was a sign of someone who was going to make a really great friend.

"So," Connor started, "…you're some kind of ninja-type?"

"No, no, no, no, no!" Nick shook his head emphatically. "Not ninja-type at all. Ninjas are a thing of the past, and kept alive by Hollywood. Sure their techniques are still around and taught, but ninjas were assassins in feudal Japan. I'm just some kid who is fortunate enough to have a dad that trained with Bruce Lee and has passed it down to me."

Connor and Wade went silent, their mouths agape. They sat there in silence and just stared at Nick.

"What? What did I say?"

Wade went first. "Dude…your dad, the guy married to your mom who is cooking spaghetti in the kitchen right now, your dad trained with BRUCE… FREAKING… LEE?!? THAT IS SO…COOL!!!"

Nick looked bemused at Wade's reaction.

"Yeah!" Connor chimed in. "Man, that is way awesome, Nick!"

Nick looked a little uncomfortable and embarrassed, which he was because he didn't like to seem like he was bragging. "Well, yeah, it is, isn't it? But again…you can't tell anybody!"

Wade looked like he was going to hyperventilate, while Connor just looked stunned. Neither one of them had ever thought that Nick's secret was this awesome!

Then they came back down to earth. "Wait a sec," Connor said. "If this is such a secret, then why are you telling us? I mean, you've only known us for a few weeks, right?"

"I am telling you this for a number of reasons. First: you came to my aid when you thought I was going to get pummeled by Zack. That shows me that you have good character.

"Second: you befriended me and didn't treat me like an annoyance, and through our friendship I can see that the both of you are true friends and understand the true meaning of friendship.

"And third: if you tell anyone," his face turned dark and serious, "I'll kick your butts so bad you won't know Friday from Christmas."

He said this last part with a sinister voice that gave Connor and Wade the creeps.

They didn't know what to say. "Uh…yeah…um…"

Nick started giggling, then laughing outright. "Kidding! Man, you guys are gullible!" He laughed so hard tears came to his eyes.

Nick and Wade started laughing as well. The friendship was quickly becoming stronger.

Nick's mom poked her head out the back door. "Boys! Dinner is ready!"

"O.K., mom! Be right there!" He turned to Connor and Wade: "Come on guys, let's eat!"

"Sweeeeet!" Wade was looking forward to it. Wade was always looking forward to food.

Connor stopped them for a moment. "Nick, dude, I'd really like to talk about this some more. What you've told us is a shock, to say the least, but I want to know more."

"Don't worry. I have a plan." He flashed that goofy grin of his, and headed towards the house. Connor and Wade followed, and dinner was served.

Chapter XIII: I Will Call You 'Grasshopper'

After dinner (which was excellent, by the way) the boys retreated to Nick's room. The sunlight was giving way to dusk and the no-see-ums were sure to be out in force looking for nice, warm bodies from which to get their evening meals.

Nick hopped up on his bed, Connor took the chair at the computer desk and Wade made himself comfortable on the floor. Nick's room was well-kept and tidy.

There were no posters hanging on the walls, no dirty clothes on the floor. The bed was made and everything seemed to be put in its proper place. The light beige walls were accentuated by the carpet which was a deeper shade of beige. There were a couple of pictures of him, his mom and his dad on the computer desk which was home to a 20" flat-screen LCD monitor for his HP computer.

"Nice room," Wade said. "...a lot neater than mine."

"I try to keep it clean, though you have come on a good day. I am not always this tidy."

"Well, your mom cooks an awesome plate of spaghetti."

"It's one of my favorites. She's good at cooking pretty much anything. Dad and I are constantly amazed at how we can go to the pantry and find absolutely nothing, and she can go in right behind us and put something together. It's uncanny."

"Speaking of your dad," Connor wondered, "where is he tonight?"

"He is teaching a class. He teaches martial-arts at his dojo."

"Your dad has his own place? Sweet. So anyway, let's get back to what we were talking about." Connor was earnest in his desire to learn more from Nick about his skills.

"I want to know more about it. The Jeet-dune, whateveryoucallit. I mean, Wade and I have taken Karate before, but we only lasted a few weeks, to tell you the truth."

"Jeet-Kune-Do."

"Right," Connor agreed. "Jeet-Kune-Do. Got it."

Nick grinned a little. "So why did you quit?"

"We found it incredibly boring. I didn't expect to become an expert right away, obviously, but it was just so, so, boring!"

"Yeah," Wade agreed. "BO-ring! I'd rather be picking fossils or surfing, dude. Much more fun."

Nick nodded in understanding. "I know. Starting out is not so exciting, but to get to the good stuff you have to learn the basics. And to learn the basics you must be focused and dedicated. It is not about having fun. It is about training one's mind and body. It is not merely a martial art, but a way of life."

Nick could see he had their rapt attention.

"In true Wing-Chun, or in any martial art for that matter, mind and body must become one, to work together. It is not something go to class for and then forget about it until the next practice. It is a way of life that you adopt that becomes a part of you as you become a part of it."

Connor and Wade sat and digested this information. For a moment they forgot they were talking to a fellow eighth-grader. It felt like Nick had, for just a bit, become a teacher…no, a *mentor*.

"I want to learn." The words just tumbled out of Connor's mouth. He was as surprised to hear them as were Wade and Nick, who both stared at him as if he had grown a third eye smack-dab in the middle of his forehead, like the alien on that Twilight Zone episode from the 60s he loved to watch.

Nick considered his friend momentarily before speaking. "You want to learn…what, exactly?"

"I want to learn Jeet-Kune-Do, like you. I want the skills, the abilities, which you have."

"Now Connor, don't make rash decisions just becau…"

Connor cut him short. "I'm not making a rash decision. I want to learn. Can you teach me?" The look on his face told Nick that he was serious.

Nick rested his chin on his hands. "Why do you want to learn? For revenge against Zack? To show off to your friends? Why do you want to learn?" For an eighth grader Nick was remarkably astute.

Connor paused before answering, gathering his thoughts together. "Not for revenge against Zack, not at all. And not to show off. I'm not a showoff."

"Then why?" Nick persisted.

"Look. I don't know if you noticed, but I have a tendency to get involved in situations that are prone to get me, and my friends…" he motioned towards Wade, "…into dangerous situations. Situations where I can get hurt."

Nick laughed at that. "HA! No, Connor. I didn't notice at all!"

"Nick! I'm serious! I want to be able to defend not just myself, but others as well! If I had even one-half the ability you have I wouldn't have to worry about Zack, or any of the other buttheads that think they can roll over me, and my friends, just because they're bigger and stronger."

Nick and Wade grew quiet, listening to Connor spill his guts.

"I mean, I hate not being able to make a difference, you know? I mean, yeah, I stand up for myself, but I get my tail kicked every time! I want to be able to stand up for myself, and for others!"

Wade poked his friend. "Dude, I never knew you were that passionate about it. I mean, I knew you were a screwball, tangling with Zack and all, but I didn't realize how much it meant to you, man."

Connor was momentarily embarrassed. "Well, it does mean a lot to me. It's not right that these guys get to run around and take our stuff and embarrass us and make us look like idiots all the time, as if they're our lords and masters. That's a load of crap!"

Nick still had his chin in his hands. "That, my friend, was the right answer."

"Huh?"

Nick sat upright, grinning broadly. "If you had answered any other way, I would tell you to pound sand. But I can see that your heart is true, and up to the task."

Connor smiled at that. "You think so?"

"Oh, yes, absolutely. I would be honored to teach you the art."

"Sweeeet! When do we start?"

"Hold on, big guy. I need to talk to my dad. I can teach you some, but my dad is the true teacher. But I need to warn you…don't start what you cannot finish. It will be lots of hard work, lots of tedious exercises, and lots of practice. It is not for the weak at heart, mind, or character; however it will fortify all three of those things. So consider that."

"I have. I want to do it. I'll do whatever it takes, Nick. I won't disappoint you, or your dad."

Nick got a playful look on his face. "That is good to know. So, then, I shall call you 'grasshopper.'"

"Huh? Grasshopper?" Connor was bemused.

"Well, in America the going gag is that any student of martial arts is called 'grasshopper.' How it came to be, I don't know. Hollywood, I'm guessing. Who am I to ruin a good joke?"

Connor laughed. "Fine. 'Grasshopper' it shall be!"

Nick grinned again, and then cut his eyes towards Wade. "And how about you, dude? Do you want to learn as well?"

"Yeah, Wade…" Connor grabbed his friend's shoulder. "C'mon, man. This is too awesome to pass up!"

"Uh…well, I suppose so."

"No!" Nick got serious once again. "There is no 'suppose so.' There is no try. Do…or do not."

Connor had heard that line somewhere before…where had he…? Oh, right. Yoda talking to Luke in "The Empire Strikes Back." Funny.

"Aw, man, I don't know…"

"Wade, dude, come on. You and me, and Nick. We can finally control our own lives, not have to worry about who is gonna screw with us each day, you know?"

"O.K. Tell you what, Wade. You sleep on it tonight, let me know tomorrow. I don't want you getting into something you don't want to do. If you don't feel like it's for you, then fine. No big.

"As for you, my friend," he looked directly at Connor, "...come over tomorrow morning and we'll introduce you to dad, O.K.?"

"Alright! I'll be here. What time?"

Nick thought for a moment. "How about ten o'clock? Dad is always up early, so that will give him time to do his morning routine. I'll let him know you're coming over." He looked at Wade. "And possibly two." He flashed that grin that Connor and Wade had become accustomed to over the past few weeks.

"Sure thing. We'll be here without fail. Thanks, Nick. This is gonna be great!"

"And I'll let you know something in the morning, too."

"Great! So it's settled, then."

The three boys got up and exited Nick's room. The wound their way to the front door, saying good-bye to Mrs. Soji and thanking her again for the (excellent) dinner she had prepared for them.

"Ten o'clock tomorrow, without fail."

"I assure you I will be here. Don't worry about that."

"I'll be here as well," Wade said.

"Great! See you in the morning!"

****

It was dark as Connor and Wade made their way home. The street lamps cast an orange, hazy glow on the sidewalk. The moon had just begun to rise over the trees behind their houses, casting them in a gloomy silhouette.

"Man, this is gonna be awesome! I can't wait to meet Nick's dad."

Wade remained silent for a moment. "What do you think, dude? Should I do this, or what?"

"What do you mean do I think you should do it? OF COURSE I think you should do it! We'd be like, like, heck, I don't know. But think of what we could do with this!"

Wade looked puzzled. "What do you mean?"

"I mean, imagine…we'd be able to finally put an end to Zack's reign, you know?"

"Dude, I thought you said this wasn't about revenge against Zack."

"It's not…I don't mean it in that way. But just think, the next time he decided to play drums with our heads, and there will be a next time, imagine the surprise he'll get when we're not so easy to pick on. I mean, he's gonna be on the warpath for us, and we need to be able to defend ourselves. It's personal for him now."

"Yeah, I know." They stopped in front of Wade's house. "Let me sleep on it. Come over in the morning and get me."

"Sure thing, ding-dong. See you in the morning." He tapped Wade on the back of the head and trotted through his front yard, disappearing into the shadows of his house cast by the concert of street lights.

Chapter XIV: Training Day

Connor was up early on Saturday morning, eager to get over to Nick's house and begin his "training." He was looking forward to meeting Mr. Soji as well. Dude trained with Bruce Lee? That in and of itself was awesome!

After getting dressed he headed downstairs for a spot of breakfast. He came through the kitchen door and started for the fridge, then noticed someone at the breakfast table. It was Wade, who was munching on a banana.

"What's up?" Wade said through a mouthful of banana.

"How long you been here, man?" Connor continued to the fridge.

"About twenty minutes, I suppose." He took a drink of OJ. "I heard you stomping around upstairs so I decided to wait for you down here. Your dad let me in."

"Ah. O.K." Connor took a carton of OJ and some strawberries his mom had sliced up from the fridge. After getting a glass from the cupboard he sat down at the table with Wade and poured himself a glass.

"So..." Connor said, "What's up?"

"You already asked me that." Wade finished his banana and tossed the peel in the garbage can.

"No, you asked me that."

"Oh, yeah. Right."

Wade finished off his OJ. He got up from the table and proceeded to the sink to wash his glass. He always cleaned up after himself, especially when at someone else's home.

"I've decided to do it. I want to do it, learn it, whatever."

"Sweet! This is gonna be great!"

Connor was pleased Wade had decided to take on the challenge with him. One, he thought it would be good for him. Two, he really didn't want to do it alone. Though Nick was a friend, their relationship was going to be one of teacher-student as opposed to that of friends.

"So what convinced you?"

"Well, a lot of things. First, I thought that it would be useful to know something like that, you know? I mean there are always going to be guys out there that are looking for nerds like us to pick on."

"This is true," Connor agreed.

"Second, I didn't want you to go through with this by yourself. The way Nick made it sound it's gonna be a lot of work, practice, you know, hard stuff. You're gonna need moral support."

Connor nodded in agreement as he took a sip of juice.

"And third, I kind of like the idea of being able to defend myself and maybe even help others, you know? I hate being helpless when someone like Zack is running the school through sheer brute force. The only reason he can do that is because no one will stand up to him, and unless the teachers catch him doing something they aren't gonna do anything to him."

"I stood up to him," Connor reminded Wade.

"I mean, almost nobody. But even though you stood up to him you couldn't do anything! Zack wiped the floor with you. I mean, sure, the other kid was spared a beating, but what good does that do? You can only do that so many times before you get seriously hurt, or before you start becoming a target, which we already have."

Connor finished his OJ as he pondered this last point. Wade was right. Bark without bite was useless, which was why he wanted to learn Jeet-Kune-Do from Nick.

"Anyway," Wade continued, "…I figured that if one person can do it would be good. Two people would be unstoppable. And we are two people, yes?"

Connor got up to wash his glass.

"Last time I checked…let me see," he pointed at Wade, "…one, two. Yep! We're two people, alright! You have a mind like a steel trap. Nothing gets by you…no sirree! You're a certifiable genius!"

"Bite me!" Wade countered.

"Hey, we need to get going. It's almost ten o'clock."

"Yeah. I'd hate to be late on our first day of 'class.' Nick might put us in the corner!"

Connor chuckled. "No kidding. Let's roll, dude."

Connor put his glass in the strainer and headed out the door as Wade followed.

****

Five minutes later they were on Nick's front porch. Wade rang the doorbell. They waited in silence for a moment as the sound of muffled thumps of footsteps could be heard coming towards the front door. Nick's mom opened the door, greeting the boys with a bright smile.

"Hello, boys! How are you? Please, come in! Nick told me you were coming."

"Thanks, Mrs. Soji." Connor still stumbled over her name and had to say it slowly as he tried to get the pronunciation correct. "Sorry," he said with a sheepish grin. His face turned a slight reddish-pink.

"Oh, that's alright. My name takes some getting used to, I know."

The boys took their shoes off before entering the house, putting them on the mat next to the front door.

"Thank you."

Nick's mom ushered them through the living room then directed them to Nick's bedroom.

"He is waiting for you. I think he is just straightening up. Nick! Your friends are here!"

Nick popped his head out from behind his bedroom door. "Hey, fellas! Whassup? Come on in! I'm just straightening up my room real quick." He disappeared back into his room as Connor and Wade started down the hallway.

They walked in to find Nick putting the finishing touches on his bed. The room looked pretty much the same as it had the night before.

"Hey, Nick." Connor stood just inside the door as Wade took up a position beside the computer desk. "Dude, what is there to straighten up? Your room looks the same as it did yesterday."

"I have to make my bed. I don't like leaving my room untidy. How someone lives tells a lot about them as a person. I keep my room neat. That shows that my life is well-ordered and short on chaos."

Wade thought of his room at home and what it looked like when he left it this morning. His bed was unmade, his clothes from the day before resting on the floor beside the clothes basket where he had thrown them. He felt embarrassed by it all of a sudden.

Nick continued. "It doesn't mean if you don't make your bed in the morning that you are a bad person, it just means your life is somewhat disordered and possibly a little chaotic. And also it instills discipline in you."

"How?" Connor couldn't see how making your bed could possibly instill discipline in someone.

"Think about it. If you cannot take three minutes in the morning to make your bed, and a couple more minutes to tidy up, then what other aspects of your life are you not giving enough time to? If you are too lazy to make your bed in the morning then how can you be expected to put the time into anything else that matters?"

"Such as…" Wade egged him on.

"Such as, say, martial arts? Remember you told me that you had taken a karate class before, but you quit because you found it to be very tedious and boring. Repetitive exercises and all that, remember?"

"Yeah, so?"

"So, if you cannot focus long enough to make your bed how are you going to be able to focus to get through the tedium of repetitive exercises? Many of those repetitive exercises will be required to hone your skills as they develop."

Connor nodded slightly. "I see your point."

"I thought you might. Consider that lesson number one."

"Number two," Connor reminded him. "We got lesson number one Thursday, remember?"

"Oh, right." Nick agreed. "Alright, well, I'm done here. Let's hit the back yard."

"Sweet. Right behind you, ninja master."

"Oh, hush."

****

The three boys had retreated to the back yard. "So," Connor said, "…where do we start?"

"Well, first of all, I spoke to my dad and he said he'd be happy to teach you guys."

"Cool!" Wade was eager to meet Mr. Soji.

"However, he cannot be here today. He had already planned to be off with some of his buddies. But he is looking forward to meeting you both. He trusts me to get you two started."

"That's fine," Connor said. "So what are we going to do today?"

"I thought you'd never ask!" Nick's face beamed as he flashed his trademark grin. "Today we will focus on what exactly is Jeet Kune Do, and we will begin to get you guys in shape. We must begin to train your bodies, as well as train your minds."

"Well, Connor and I think we're in pretty good shape. I mean, we don't lift weights or anything, but we're both fit." Wade curled his arm, flexing his bicep which was not all that noticeable.

"Uh, yeah." Nick looked at Wade, and shook his head in a pitying manner.

"What?"

"Anyway," Nick continued, "…we need to get you guys in shape. It's not about muscle, though muscle doesn't hurt. Again, look at me. Everyone judges me by my size. I'm just a skinny little Asian kid. Perfect target for bullies."

"Tell me about it." Connor said.

"Alright, then. You both should know better than to judge by size. Zack is twice my size, and he probably still doesn't know what hit him, so he probably won't bother with me again; not for awhile, anyway."

"So…again, where do we start, then?" Connor was eager to get things going.

"Well, for one thing, you need to learn patience. I know you want to learn, but you must be patient. Patience, patience, patience!"

Connor felt like a student being scolded by his teacher. Heck, that's what it was, wasn't it? He *was* the student, and Nick *was* the teacher. This was going to take some getting used to.

"Patience, check. Wade, you got that?" Connor elbowed Wade. "Patience."

"Yup! Patience! Got it!"

Nick sighed. He could tell it was going to be a long road with these guys. "You guys go home and change into running shoes and shorts. We've got some running to do."

“Aye, aye, *mon Capitan*!” Connor gave him a mock salute. Wade, following Connor’s lead, did the same. Then they both turned and sprinted for home.

Chapter XV: Ground Rules

Connor and Wade were back in ten minutes. They ran back to Nick's house and went straight to the back yard where Nick stretching in preparation for their run. Nick stopped stretching and greeted them, grinning from ear to ear. He was happy they both decided to take up the art and was looking forward to helping train them.

"You guys all ready to go?"

"Yeah. Ready, dude. Let's get started!" Wade was much more enthusiastic about the training than he was the day before.

Connor was more excited than Wade was. "Yeah…let's get going. What's first? Blocking, kicking, what?"

"Before we begin any of that we must begin to condition your minds and bodies."

"O.K. So what are we gonna do?" Wade was hopping in place, releasing some of the bound-up energy that was being generated by his enthusiasm to get started.

"You guys are in alright shape, but during the fight with Zack the other day you were on the verge of being exhausted, yes?"

Connor nodded. "Yes, we were. I mean, we're in shape, somewhat, I guess, but that fight dragged on and on. I wasn't sure how much longer I could last."

"I know. When I showed up you guys were on your last legs. You are in decent shape, but you must improve your stamina. So, first up: three mile run!"

Wade's jaw dropped. "Three miles? Are you kidding?"

"No. I am not kidding. Three miles, today and each day thereafter. For awhile, at least. As your conditioning improves we'll increase it bit by bit. I see us doing five miles in the coming weeks easy."

Wade thought he was going to die. Three miles? Then five later? What had he stepped into?

Nick noted the look of concern on Wade's face.

"What's the matter Wade? Not up to it?"

"What? I mean…well, heck yeah, I'm up to it! Let's rock and roll!" He couldn't very well lose face at this point, could he?

"Good! First, we stretch, then some push-ups and sit-ups, then some more stretching, then we run. Ready, grasshoppers?"

****

The run, along with the warm-up and the stretching, was much more intense than either Connor or Wade had anticipated. They had both struggled to keep up with Nick, who barely broke a sweat, but they held their own and completed the run.

Before the run Nick had put them through some stretches, many of which were tortuous for the other two as they hadn't stretched in quite some time.

"Don't worry," Nick said, "…you guys are still pretty limber and the stretching will get you to where you need to be for flexibility."

After the stretches they did several varieties of push-ups. First they did regular push-ups, hands shoulder-width apart. Then they did wide-stance pushups with their arms stretched out about a foot from their bodies on either side.

Finally they did diamond push-ups, where they put their hands together to form a diamond, stuck their butts in the air and brought their noses down into the center of the diamond. That was rough.

After each set of push-ups Nick had them do crunches (which were much better than sit-ups, Nick explained). All in all they did about ninety push-ups (three sets of ten of each type) and an equal amount of crunches.

Wade was tempted to say something about the brutal workout but thought better of it. After all, he had signed up for this. He wasn't forced to do anything, so better to suck it up and do what he needed to be done.

Connor and Wade were on the picnic table, heads back, as they labored to suck in enough air to curb their lungs' craving for more. Nick stood and looked at them, shaking his head in mock disdain.

"Guys, whassa matter? Can't handle it?"

Connor picked his head up and cut his eyes at Nick. "What do you mean, 'Can't handle it?'" He heaved a couple more times. "I think we did fine, for our first three-mile run." He laid his head back on the table again.

"Yeah," Wade said. "Give us a break, dude."

"Kidding!" He was grinning again. "Look, guys. You did very well. I mean, for your first three-mile run, not to mention all the exercises I put you through beforehand."

"You're telling me!" Connor said without lifting his head.

"I promise you…give it a week and you will see definite improvement in your endurance."

"What do you mean a week? You mean next week?" Wade sat up and rested his elbows on his knees, looking at Nick.

"I mean, we have to work it every day. We won't run tomorrow, to give your bodies a chance to adjust and heal. However you need to exercise every day or else you will lose what you have gained. So Monday we will do it again. If you're up to it."

Connor sat up. "Oh, we're up to it, aren't we, Wade?" He elbowed Wade in the ribs.

"Yeah. We're up to it, Nicky boy. Don't you worry about that."

"Good! Then we are through with conditioning for today, and we'll pick it up again after school on Monday, yes?"

"Yes" the other two said in unison.

"The rewards will be well worth the commitment and effort you will give, I promise."

"I sure hope so, dude." Wade stood up, put his hands on his head and began to walk around a bit, trying to ease the effects of the run.

"It will. Trust me!" There was that grin again. "Now, I want to explain what it is that you will be learning."

"Finally!" Thought Connor.

****

Nick, Connor and Wade were sitting at the picnic table after taking a five-minute break during which they all drank copious amounts of water and had a snack consisting of PB&J and fruit which included strawberries, blueberries and grapes. They were mostly rested now and their stomachs were good to go until dinner time.

"First," Nick said, "...what is Jeet Kune Do? Simply put it is the martial-arts style that was created by Bruce Lee. Specifically it means 'Way of the Intercepting Fist.' It is really a style that is all things while at the same time is nothing."

Nick looked at the bewildered looks on his friends'/students' faces as he allowed the information to sink in. "Confused?"

"Uh, yeah, as a matter of fact." Wade rubbed the back of his head as if the strain of trying to wrap his head around this concept made his head hurt.

Nick continued. "Bruce Lee himself stated that he had not created a new style. Instead he said that his intention was to free those who studied Jeet Kune Do from clinging to any one style. Jeet Kune Do incorporates Wing Chun Kung Fu, American-style boxing, jujitsu, karate, and fencing."

"Fencing?" Connor's head perked up.

"Yes, fencing. Think about it: fencing has many moves that are very complimentary to the martial arts. Most people, especially here in the United States, when you mention martial arts they immediately think of nothing more than fight scenes from the movies. High kicks, lots of blocks, and a lot of smacking noises. That's not what the martial arts are. The martial arts are just that: art.

"Yes, the martial arts are great fighting techniques, but they are, first and foremost, an art. Jeet Kune Do takes the best out of these different fighting styles and incorporates them into one fluid art."

The look on Connor's face showed that Nick had gotten his point across. "So, we are going to learn parts of different fighting styles and make them our own? Kind of like a recipe?"

"Exactly!" Nick's face beamed with glee. "You understand!"

"I don't know," Wade said. "It sounds like a lot to learn. I mean, how are we going to learn five or six different skills? Those take a long time to learn."

"You are missing the point. Like Connor said, it is like a recipe. If you bake a cake you use sugar, right?"

"Right."

"It is not necessary that you know how to make sugar, it is just there. You add that to the cake batter to make the cake. It is the same with Jeet Kune Do. It is not necessary to learn all of these techniques, just the best parts. Yes, it will take some time, but with practice and determination you will put it all together. My dad is an excellent teacher."

"When do we get to meet him, by the way?" Connor was eager to meet Mr. Soji.

"Yeah," Wade agreed. "When do we meet your dad?"

Nick took a seat on the picnic table next to Connor. "Sometime in the coming week. For now I just want you guys to read up on Jeet Kune Do over the weekend to get a little more familiar with it. It is going to take some time but we'll get there, promise!"

"Sweeeeet." Connor was ready to become a martial arts master, and he was willing to do whatever it took to get there. "I'm committed. Make me a fighting machine, little master."

"We will. Have patience, fellas. With that, class for today is over, to be continued on Monday after school. Be here, or be somewhere else. We'll do the same thing we did today and then break for dinner and homework. After that maybe we'll get a little more in-depth about Jeet Kune Do, and we can talk about what you guys read. O.K.?"

"O.K.!" Wade was getting his enthusiasm back and was as eager as Connor to continue training with Nick. He was especially eager to meet Mr. Soji.

"Great! So, what now?"

"Who's up for a swim?" Wade offered. His parents had put in an above-ground pool before the warm weather arrived. "The pool is ready to go, and it's really warm out here."

"Count me in!" Nick loved to swim. "Let me run and get my trunks real quick. I'll be right back!" He jumped up from the table and ran inside.

He was back in two minutes, trunks on and goggles in hand. "Let's boogie!"

"Boogie? Really, dude?" Wade and Connor both got up. They came around the house and took a left turn onto the sidewalk towards Wade's house.

"Hey, Nick," Conner began. "We really appreciate you doing this. I mean, this is really cool and all, but we realize you are giving up some of your time, and so is your dad. Wade and I really appreciate it."

“I know you do. Thanks for telling me. But if I thought you were going to not follow through or if I thought your intentions were other than good I wouldn’t have offered.”

“Well, thanks again.”

They arrived at Wade’s house. Connor ran to his house to change into his swim suit as Wade ran into his house to do the same. Nick sat on the pool deck and waited.

They were back in a matter of minutes. The remainder of the day was spent swimming…and strengthening the bonds of friendship.

Chapter XVI: Meeting Dad

Connor and Wade headed straight to Nick's house right after school. They decided to take the long route, again, to ensure that they would avoid Zack.

He had been back at school today and it took all of their wiles to avoid being seen by him, but they survived the day. Zack didn't have his arm in a sling and he wasn't favoring it so the two of them figured the damage was minimal, though probably still fresh in his head, which meant danger for them.

The run was more brutal today. The workout that Nick had put them through on Saturday had been tough on their bodies and they were still sore and stiff from using muscles they had never used before. To further exacerbate their conditions Nick had put them through more stretches and more exercises today than he had on Saturday ("Saturday was just a warm up…" he had said with a grin).

The stretching regimen, along with the push-ups of various types, crunches, and squats had served to totally wipe out Connor and Wade, who now lay on Nick's front yard, convinced they were going into cardiac arrest.

"Guys, get up! It is not good to sit still after a run! Get up and walk around! Put your hands on your heads or on your hips. Walk it off!"

Connor pushed himself up off the grass. As he stood up he offered his hand to Wade and helped him up as well. They did as Nick said and put their hands above their heads as they walked around the yard. Their breaths were labored and deep, but that began to subside as they walked around.

"Good!" Nick smiled. He was not breathing heavily at all much to Connor's amazement. "After we rest up and get rehydrated we'll sit down and go over some things."

"Yeah…" Wade was still walking with his hands over his head. "Good idea. We'll sit down. Awesome. I like that idea."

"Awwww…whassa matter, Wade? Too much?"

"What? No, dude, not too much. It's just…it's just that…" Wade was still breathing heavily. "…it's just that I…thought I was…in better…shape. Dude."

"Well, apparently not, *dude*. That's why I am pushing you to your limits. Once you have reached your limits, we will stretch those limits to points you never thought possible. You are going to endure things you never thought you were capable of. You are going to be one fit, trim fighting machine."

Connor had stopped walking and was now bent over with his hands on his knees. "Really? And just how far are we going to push those limits, Nick?"

"As far as we can. If you want to be able to defend yourself, you must be able to outlast your opponent. Not every adversary you will face is going to be as clumsy as Zack.

"You must face every opponent with the mind-set that they may be more skilled than you and in better shape than you. You need to be in peak physical shape at all times, and you must have a much higher threshold for physical endurance, and pain, than everyone else."

"O.K. I'll keep that in mind when the paramedics get here to shock me back to life." Wade had stopped walking and was now standing next to Connor who was still bent over with his hands on his knees.

"You'll be fine. Come on. Let's head out back and sit down."

"Awesome." Connor was finally breathing normally again, though Wade was still catching his breath even as his breathing had almost returned to normal as well.

They walked around to the rear of the house and planted themselves on the picnic table that they were getting so familiar with. There was a slight breeze blowing which helped to cool their sweat-soaked bodies. They sat quietly for a moment as the cool air enveloped them, thankful for the brief respite.

Connor had a momentary urge to run to Wade's house and jump in the pool, but that wouldn't be cool, especially since he was covered in sweat and wearing sweat-soaked clothes.

"Alrighty, then..." Nick began, but stopped short as the back door of the house opened. They all turned to look. It was Nick's dad, Mr. Soji. One look and you could definitely tell which parent Nick took his features from.

Mr. Soji was a smallish man, about five feet two inches tall, slender with a slight build. He had a mop of jet-black hair which framed his face, which had an air of serenity about it. He had small brown eyes which sparkled with intensity and...of course...the grin.

Mr. Soji stepped out from the door and headed over towards the boys sitting at the picnic table. "Hello, boys! How are you?"

They all stood up and turned towards him. "Dad, these are my friends. This is Connor," he motioned to Connor, "…and Wade. These are the two I told you about."

"Well, hello, Connor, Wade." He shook each of their hands. For such a small man he sure had one heckuva grip. Not bone-crushing, but you could tell there was incredible strength there.

"Hello to you both. I am glad to finally meet you. Okita has told me much about you. I am looking forward to assisting in your training."

Connor spoke up. "Well, we appreciate you allowing us to train, Mr. Soji. We are looking forward to it as well."

"Yes sir," Wade chimed in. "We really, really appreciate it."

"It is my pleasure. I just hope you are both up to the challenge. It is going to take lots of hard work and determination. There will be days you don't want to train, and you must force yourself to do it. There will be days when nothing can keep you from your exercises and all goes right. But every day, train you must."

This last line struck Connor as Yoda-like, and he had to stifle a giggle as he envisioned the tiny green Jedi master, pointy ears and bulging eyes, instructing him in the ways of the Force:

"Every day, train you must. Judge me by my size, do you? Hmmm?"

He had to laugh. He faked a coughing fit to hide it.

“My goodness, are you alright, Connor?” Mr. Soji put a hand on his shoulder.

“Oh yeah…” he said between (fake) coughs. “Must have been some pollen, or a gnat, or something went down my throat. That’s all. Thank you.”

He patted him on the back once more and stepped away. “Well, it was good to meet you both. Based on what Nick has told me about you I think you are both going to make excellent students. I am looking forward to you beginning training. Speaking of which, when will you be starting at the dojo?”

Connor looked at Wade. “Uh, well, we need to talk to our parents first. We’d like to start this week, if that’s alright.”

“Well, I have instructed Nick to shape you both up a little first, before you come for your first lesson.”

“Oh. O.K. then. Well, I guess that’s up to Nick…?” Connor and Wade both turned to Nick, inquisitive looks on their faces.

“Well, dad, they’re actually in pretty good shape. They just need some minor conditioning for now. They’ll be good by the end of the week, I think. Not perfect, but good enough.”

“Ah, then, you may start next week. O.K.?”

“Awesome! That’s great!” Connor was elated. He turned to Wade. “Ain’t that great, Wade?”

“Yeah, dude. Totally. I can’t wait to start.”

“Well, I am looking forward to you starting. We will plan to begin next Monday, provided your parents are agreeable, yes?”

"Thank you Mr. Soji. That would be fantastic." Connor extended his hand, which Mr. Soji took. Wade followed suit.

"Yes, sir. Thank you again. We'll make you proud."

"I should hope so…" he said with a smile. "We'll see you soon."

"Yes, sir," they said in unison.

With that, Mr. Soji turned and started for the house. Connor noticed the confidence in his walk. He wasn't cocky, that wasn't it at all. Mr. Soji seemed to be very humble and soft-spoken. But you could tell a lot about a person from the way they carried themselves and Nick's dad carried himself well. He made a mental note to work on his posture.

After Mr. Soji disappeared into the house Nick turned back to Connor and Wade. "Well, what did you think?"

Wade spoke first. "Dude, totally not what I expected."

"Really?" Nick sounded puzzled. "What did you expect?"

This caught Wade off-guard somewhat. He hadn't thought about it, really. "You know, I don't know, actually. You sure take after your dad, though. You guys look a lot alike."

"Yeah," Connor agreed. "You two could almost pass for each other if it wasn't for the fact that your dad has thirty years on you. He seems really nice. I hope we size up to his expectations."

“I am sure you will. He is hard to please, but he is fair and will do anything for you if he knows you are giving your best effort. He is a great teacher.”

“Well, anyone who trained with Bruce Lee back in the day has to be a great teacher. Wouldn’t you agree, ding-dong?” Wade gave a playful push to Connor.

“Heck yeah, man. I am excited. I can hardly wait to start!” Connor began to bounce up and down on the balls of his feet.

“Well, we continue conditioning this week and if all goes well then we start next Monday.”

“Sweeeet…” Connor flashed a broad grin.

“Alright, guys. I have homework to get to, so I have to go in.”

“Yeah, me too,” Connor said. “I’m in the middle of a ten-page report that’s due on Friday.”

“Not me, dudes. Did my homework in class.”

“Sweet. You can come over and help me with my paper.”

“Wha…? Aw, man!”

“Alright, Nick. We’ll talk to you later. Let’s go, ding-dong!”

“Later, guys.” Nick disappeared through the back door as the other two trudged off to Connor’s house.

Chapter XVII: The Unexpected

It was early Monday morning when Connor was awakened by a tapping at his bedroom window. He opened one eye, waited, didn't hear anything, and rolled back over, figuring it was a dream. Just as he was about to drift back into unconsciousness…

BANG! BANG! BANG! BANG!

The banging jolted him awake. He sat upright, jumped out of bed and stumbled to the window. Looking outside he didn't see anything…

The face appeared suddenly and out of nowhere, pressing against his window creating a grotesque sight.

"GAAAHHH! What the crap…!?"

He fell backwards on the floor. It scared him enough that he almost lost control of his bodily functions. And then he heard the giggling.

"Connor, you awake?"

"Who the…?" He got up and walked back over to the window. Looking out he saw…

"Nick?" He opened the window and stuck his head out. "Nick? What are you doing, man? Are you nuts? Do you know what time it is? It's…uh…" He turned to look at his clock. "It's, like, four o'clock in the morning, man!"

"I know. Good morning, sunshine! Are you ready?"

"Ready for what? I'm not supposed to be awake for another two hours! Jeez! What the heck am I supposed to be ready for?"

“Today begins the next step in training. From here it gets more intense. Today we are going to dad’s dojo for your first day of training, and so today we begin our early-morning exercise routine, so get your shorts and shoes and let’s rock-n-roll!”

“ARE…YOU…OUT…OF…YOUR…MIND?!?!” Connor said this as loud as he could whisper without waking his parents.

“If you will remember, you agreed to do as I asked when it came to training. This is part of that. You did not expect to be woken at four a.m. for an exercise session, yes?”

“Yeah. So?”

“You must be prepared for the unexpected. When the unexpected happens you must be able to assess the situation and react accordingly. This is unexpected. Now you must react accordingly, namely getting your running gear on and getting out here.”

Connor put his head down on the window sill hard enough to create a muffled “THUMP” as his head made contact with the wood, causing the window to vibrate slightly.

“Criminy, man.” He took a deep breath and resigned himself to his fate. “Alright, Nick. I’m coming. Five minutes.”

“Good! Let me go get Wade and we’ll be ready to go! Oh, and don’t eat anything. It will give you cramps. Just water. You can eat when you get back, alright?”

“Whatever. I’ll meet you in front of Wade’s house.”

“Hurry. You have three minutes.”

“Five.”

Connor shut his window as Nick skulked off into the morning to repeat the process with Wade.

He had to be insane. That was it…yeah. He's insane. Connor decided, at that moment, that he and Wade had placed their lives in the hands of an insane thirteen-year-old with an incredibly warped mind. An insane thirteen-year-old who knew Jeet-Kune-Do and could wipe the floor with both of them.

Wonderful.

****

The run that morning wasn't so bad, aside from the fact that Nick woke them up at four-frickin'-a.m. They were getting faster and the soreness had all but disappeared as their bodies got used to the regimen of running, stretching, and exercises that Nick was putting them through.

The run took about twenty minutes, which isn't bad for a three mile jaunt. Together with the stretching and exercises total time was about one hour. That made it about five o'clock which gave the boys over an hour to get ready for school.

Nick was just as cheerful as ever, even at this hour of the morning. Well, Connor thought, the boy was insane, so naturally he's all chipper at all hours of the day. It just wasn't natural.

"Alright, guys. We'll meet here after school, get any homework done and then we'll head to the dojo for your first lesson."

“Cool. How’re we gonna get there? My mom could drive us, I suppose.” Connor’s mom was always willing to drive the boys if she was available.

“No, that will not be necessary.”

“Is your mom gonna take us?” Wade asked.

“Nope."

"So," Connor began, "…how are we going to get there?"

"We will run. That will be our afternoon workout. The gym is about two miles from here. Two miles there, two miles back, that gives us four miles. It should only take about fifteen minutes each way.”

“Dude, you are going to kill us! Three runs a day? You’re insane!” Wade was clearly not happy about the travel arrangements.

“Look, guys.” Nick put on his understanding face. “We are going to be doing two runs per day, and I was going to increase the afternoon workout to four miles anyway. If you guys really want to be as good as you say you do, and if you really want to be as good as you can be, this is necessary.

"I am not doing this just to do it. It has a purpose. There is a point to it. Trust me, alright? You guys have improved greatly in just one week! Don’t get discouraged. It will be worth it.”

Nick put his best “trust me” smile on, and honestly, Connor thought, how could you not trust him? They were friends after all, and he didn’t have to offer to train them.

“Alright. We put our lives in your hands, even if you are certifiably insane. Right, Wade?”

“Yeah. Sure. I’m in it for the long haul, dude.”

“Great! I’ll see you guys here after school.”

Nick disappeared around the corner of his house as Connor and Wade began walking back to their houses.

"Dude, what have we gotten ourselves into?" Wade was not expecting to have to put so much into the training. "He's nuts, man! Workouts at four-o'clock in the morning? Cripes!"

"Oh, quit your whining. He knows what he's doing. We agreed to do what he asked of us, and this is one of those things. We knew going into this it was going to be intense."

"Yeah, but not this intense! What's he gonna do next? Have us rappelling from helicopters to the top of the school building? Jeez!"

"Just bear with it, Wade. Like you said: we're in it for the long haul. I'm not gonna quit, and neither are you. We can do this. We want to do this."

"Yeah, you're right. Anyway, let's get ready for school. I'll be over in a bit."

"Cool. See you then."

They ran to their respective houses. In the back of his mind Connor did have a nagging doubt about his ability to see this through, but he quickly put it away. Nothing was going to deter him from his goal. He was sure of that.

He knew he could take this on. He had to take this on. There was no choice. If he pulled out now he would look like a quitter, not to mention he would disappoint Wade and Nick, and hadn't he talked Wade into doing this with him?

What's more, he would forever be at the mercy of that jerk, Zack. No, there was no stopping now.

Something else he was sure of was that there were going to be some definite lifestyle changes if he were going to survive this. That was certain.

He crept into his house and stole quietly to his bedroom to prepare for the day ahead.

Chapter XVIII: Training Day (Finally!)

Connor and Wade went straight to Nick's house after school as they had discussed. Nick was already home and waiting on his buddies.

"Wassup, guys? Ready for your first day of training?"

"Heck, yeah, we are! I thought the school day would never end!" Wade's enthusiasm level for learning Jeet Kune Do had grown significantly over the past week. The exercise regimen that Nick was putting them through had helped him to see that he could push his limits beyond what he thought possible and his confidence level rose accordingly.

"Yeah. Let's get this party started, little master."

Connor had dismissed his initial doubts. Having to skirt the neighborhood on the way home from school helped. He resented having to sneak about trying to avoid Zack. He felt like a prisoner trying to evade capture. Every day he had to do this just steeled his resolve even more. "Let's hit it."

****

The run to the dojo was quick. It was only two miles from the neighborhood and they covered the distance in twelve minutes, quite an improvement from when they started a little more than a week ago.

Running into Zack was a concern. However with three of them running together it was highly unlikely Zack would engage them, especially with Nick present.

They took a quick breather upon arriving at Mr. Soji's dojo. When they walked in the dojo seemed empty. It was a nice place, not fancy at all, but simple, clean, and tidy.

It was obviously well taken care of. There was some equipment including a punching bag and a speed bag in the far corner off to the right. There were thick, blue mats on the floor where practice took place, obviously there to cushion falls. A Japanese flag hung on the wall to the left while the American flag hung from the wall in the back.

"Hey, guys, take off your shoes, o.k.?"

"I thought that was at home, dude."

"You must remove your shoes before entering the dojo. It is a sign of respect."

"Got it."

Connor and Wade both removed their shoes and put them by the front door.

Connor was looking around when he saw the picture of Bruce Lee hanging next to the front door. He walked over to it to get a better look. It was a still shot from the movie "Enter the Dragon." Bruce was looking off to his side, one hand up towards his chin, the other next to his hip. It was a pretty awesome shot, done in black and white.

On the bottom was an inscription: "To Hideki Soji. One of my better students. Bruce Lee." The signature was pretty stylized.

"Hello?" Nick called out. "Hello? Dad?"

It was very quiet in the building. Suddenly Mr. Soji appeared from a door in the back of the room.

"Boys! Hello! Come, come!" Mr. Soji motioned with his arm for them to come to him. Connor broke away from the picture and headed towards Nick's dad with the other two.

"Hey, dad! We're here right on time."

"Good. I am glad you all made it alright. Hello, Connor. Hello, Wade. Are you ready to begin training today?"

Connor began to answer when Wade cut him off.

"I'll say we are! I am pumped!"

"Pumped, eh? Well, good! We'll get started in a bit."

"Where is everyone else, Mr. Soji?" Connor asked.

"No classes until five. You boys are getting a class all to yourselves."

"Really? Neat!" Wade thought that was really cool. "Well, we talked to our parents, and they're cool with everything. We just need to know how much it's gonna cost us and…"

Mr. Soji waved his hand and shook his head. "Don't worry about cost. You boys are no charge."

"Really?" Connor looked at Wade, then Nick, and then back at Mr. Soji. "Aw, sir, we couldn't expect to…"

Mr. Soji waved his hand again. "No! No charge! No argument! You are Okita's friends, and as such you are welcome in my dojo, and my home, any time. I only have two conditions."

Connor and Wade stared at Mr. Soji. "Yes, sir?"

He had a stern, serious look about him as he spoke. "Condition number one: you give one hundred percent to your training. There will be days where you must do things you do not want to do. There will be days you don't want to practice. There will be days you will want to just give up and wonder why you are here. Please, do not waste my time and yours. If you begin the instruction, you give it your all. Agreed?"

"Yes, sir," they said in unison.

"Condition number two: as you progress you will become more and more skilled obviously. These skills are not to be flaunted about and are not to be used for any purpose other than self-defense or defense of those unable to defend themselves. You do not pick fights. You do not show off. Nobody is to know about your skills. Agreed?"

"Yes, sir," they said in unison again while nodding their heads.

His face remained stern for a moment, and then he broke into a wide grin. "Excellent! Then we begin shortly. Nick, get them ready, O.K.?"

"O.K. dad." He turned to Connor and Wade. "You guys ready?"

Connor took off his shoes. "Does a bear poop in the woods? Heck yeah! Let's do this!"

"Yeah," Wade agreed. "I've never been so ready."

"Good! First up: fifty push-ups, on the knuckles!"

****

After their warm-up they sat down on the floor and waited for Mr. Soji, who came into the dojo after about three minutes. As he entered they all stood up.

Mr. Soji took his spot in front of the three boys. "Now, we begin. First, some rules.

"Rule number one: be prompt. I do not tolerate tardiness.

"Second: always bow upon entering the dojo. Direct your bow towards the senior person, which in most, if not all, cases will be me.

"Third: behave appropriately when in the dojo. That means you remove your shoes before entering, no chewing gum, no cell phones, no games, and no eating or drinking. These are not allowed in my dojo.

"Fourth: Pay attention. If you are not paying attention you are not learning. If you are not learning you are wasting my time. I do not like having my time wasted. It is disrespectful. Pay attention.

"Fifth: Never lose your temper during practice. I say during practice, but extend that to your life outside the dojo as well. Never let me hear about you losing your temper. It is unnecessary and counterproductive.

"And finally: Practice your skills every day outside of class, even if it is only for a few minutes a day. This is the only way you will improve your skills. In the morning when you wake, practice. In the evening before you sleep, practice. During the day when you have nothing else to do, practice.

"That is all, for now. Do you have any questions?"

Connor raised his hand. "When do you expect us to have our ghis?" A ghi is the traditional uniform worn when practicing martial arts consisting of a heavy cotton top, secured with a belt, and heavy cotton trousers. The uniform is loose-fitting to allow for greater mobility when practicing.

"By next practice. Definitely."

"Oh. O.K." Connor put his hand down.

"No more questions? Good! Let's begin.

"Now, before we start instruction, we will bow. Bowing is a show of respect and humility. If you wish to gain respect, you must first show respect. Respect is earned, not given.

"When you bow your feet should be at a forty-five degree angle, your hands should be at your sides, palms towards your hips, and you will bow from the waist. Let's try it together."

Nick gave a picture-perfect bow, which was expected. Connor put his feet together but let his hands hang in front of him. Wade bowed so deeply he almost fell over.

"Not bad, but you will need practice. Okita, you must teach them proper technique."

"Yes, sir."

"Good. Now, when we are here in the dojo I am your sensei, which means 'teacher.' So anytime you wish to address me, you will address me as 'sensei.' Understood?"

"Yes, sir," Connor and Wade said together.

"Apparently not. Understood?"

Connor and Wade looked at each other, when the light bulb came on. They turned back towards Mr. Soji. "Yes, sensei."

"Good. You boys catch on quickly. Now we will begin your first lesson."

****

They took positions on the floor, cross-legged. The three boys sat side-by-side facing their sensei. Even though Nick sat with Connor and Wade he was going to be a teacher, not a student. For the time being, however, he would sit with them and listen to his dad.

Mr. Soji sat silent for a moment, and then began. "So, here we are." He looked over his pupils, sizing them up before beginning his lesson.

"What is Jeet Kune Do? Connor? Do you know the answer?"

Connor's face flushed as he was not expecting a pop quiz. "Well, it is a martial art."

Mr. Soji kept his gaze on him waiting for him to continue. "Go on."

"Uh...well, it is a martial art, but not just a martial art. It is, if I understand it correctly, a combination of martial arts as well as different types of techniques from all over. I think Nick said that it included boxing, and...fencing?"

Sensei nodded in approval. "Very good, Connor. And Wade? What is your take on Jeet Kune Do?"

Wade fidgeted a bit before answering, scratching his forehead as if to draw the answer to the front of his brain where it would just fall out of his mouth.

"Well, pretty much what Connor said. I know it was developed by Bruce Lee, who you trained under, and that it incorporates many different fighting styles."

"Excellent. Nick has done well with you both."

Nick seemed nonplussed by the praise. "Thank you, sensei." Nick bowed slightly as he said it.

“What is Jeet Kune Do? Literally, it means ‘the way of the intercepting fist.’ As Master Bruce would have said, it is everything, and it is nothing.”

Connor and Wade showed puzzled looks, but they did not say anything.

“Confused?”

“Yes, sensei.” Connor said. And he was confused! “How can something be everything and nothing?”

“In a nutshell, Connor, the Jeet Kune Do disciple studies many different styles, taking the best of those styles and makes them one. Does that make sense?”

“A little.”

“In other words, we take some components of karate, some components of judo, some components of tae-kwon-do, some components of western-style boxing, and some components of fencing.

“No art is superior to any other. To have no limitation is the only limitation. Do not cling to any set pattern, any rigid catalog of moves. You are what you become, and that, my young students, is what Jeet-Kune-Do is all about.

“However, for our purposes here, at least to start, we will be learning the tenets of Wing Chun Kung Fu. You are too inexperienced to totally understand the meaning of Jeet Kune Do so we will focus on Wing Chun to give you a basis from which to work. When you have become proficient in Wing Chun we will move on to other styles.

“As we focus on Wing Chun we will also incorporate boxing and while we will not learn fencing we will learn the basics. These three techniques will form the basis of your skills.

"In the coming weeks and months you will learn many different techniques, all of which will serve to help you evolve into skilled martial artists. Now…do you have any questions?"

The boys remained silent.

"No? Good. Now then, Connor…what is your purpose for wanting to learn martial arts?"

"My purpose?"

"Yes, your purpose. Why are you here? What has driven you to be here today? There is something that has brought you here."

"Well, I guess 'cause I'm tired of being picked on. I want to be able to defend myself if I need to."

Mr. Soji raised an eyebrow as if he expected more. And he did expect more. "That's not why you are here. Close your eyes and delve deep into your conscience and tell me why you are really here."

Connor did as he was told and closed his eyes and inhaled deeply as if meditating. They all sat in silence.

Mr. Soji turned to Wade. "Wade, why are you here? What brought you here today?"

"Well, sensei, to be honest I hadn't even considered it until we met your son, and even then Connor had to talk me…"

Mr. Soji waved his hand and shook his head. "No, no. That's not what I am looking for. You close your eyes and do as Connor is doing. Do not tell me why you came here; tell me why you are here!"

They sat in silence momentarily. Suddenly Connor's eyes popped open and he drew another deep breath.

“Sensei. What has brought me here? O.K., I want to be able to defend myself, yes. I am tired of being picked on. I am tired of having to run around avoiding certain people for fear of getting my head caved in.

“However it is not just me. I am tired of watching as my friends and classmates endure the same torture. I am tired of bullies being able to walk around with impunity, causing trouble at will with whoever they want whenever they want.

“I want to be able to help others as well. What good is this awesome ability if you can’t use it for anything? How selfish is that? I’m always getting involved in situations I know I should steer clear of but poke my nose in anyway. Wade can vouch for me on that.”

Wade snapped his eyes open. “Yes, sir. That’s true, I can promise you.”

“Anyway,” Connor continued, “…I want to…I don’t know. I had this dream, thought, fantasy, whatever you want to call it, that I could learn this and perhaps, maybe, I don’t know…” He stopped suddenly, as if he didn’t want to say what came next.

“Go on…” Mr. Soji encouraged him. “What is it?”

“Look. Imagine what the three of us could do if we were able to use this to help others. I don’t mean running around picking fights, but looking out for others and for each other. If someone is getting their head pounded in we can help.

"I guess, kind of, I had this vision of ninjas, where we dart in, kick some ass, dart back out before the bad guys ever knew what hit them. Excuse me, sensei, I mean, kick some butt.”

“You are excused, Connor. I understand your excitement.”

“Sensei Soji,” Wade piped up, “…when Connor first mentioned this to me, taking martial arts, I mean, he had to talk me into it. He was so excited about it! I wasn’t. But the more I thought about it, the more I liked the idea as well. I’m tired of the bullies too.

"I’m here because my best friend dragged me into it, but I remained here because I want to learn as well. I’m here for the duration, sir, and I agree with Connor that we can do this.”

“Hey,” Nick interjected. “…what about me? I mean, I’m part of this too, ain’t I?”

“Well, we didn’t want to speak for you, man. I mean, we never really talked about it, ya’ know?”

“Well, I’m in. If it’s O.K. with my dad, that is.”

Mr. Soji allowed a smile to creep across his face.

“Well. Big dreams for such youngsters. Your hearts are pure and your actions show your character.”

Connor looked surprised. “Our actions?”

“Yes. Nick told me about the day you intervened to help him. You didn’t have to do that. You could have just walked past, giving no thought to the situation. But you didn’t. That tells me much about your spirit, your soul, what is in your hearts. That is what I was looking for.”

They sat for another moment before Mr. Soji spoke again. “So it will be. Fine. Yes. So it will be. As for your dream of being a team, that is something we must save for discussion at a later time.”

The boys were all smiling, proud to be at the start of something that, they hoped, would be a force for good. Connor just hoped he could learn everything.

"Well, if we are to make this a reality, there must be some understandings. Listen closely, and carefully."

"Yes, sensei." The three boys sounded like a small choir as they spoke in unison.

"First: as we discussed before, you are not to flaunt your abilities. Nobody is to know about them, and if you do have to use them you use only the force that is necessary and no more.

"The first rule of combat: never reveal your strengths, lest your opponent be able to prepare to counter them. Never reveal your weaknesses lest your opponent know how to exploit them. No showboating! This isn't the NFL, and you aren't wide receivers making the game-winning catch. Understood?"

"Yes, sensei!"

"Second: you work as a team. None of you is above the other. None of you is better than the other. Nobody does anything without the approval of the team and your sensei, which is me. Understood?"

"Yes, sensei!"

"Third: you will give one hundred percent in all your training, but you must not neglect your everyday life. Your homework, your housework, your family. These are all important, especially your family. Jeet Kune Do should become your way of life without becoming your life. Understood?"

"Yes, sensei!"

"Good! Now, as for the schedule. You will run straight here from school each day, Monday through

Friday, for your workout and lessons. On Saturdays we will practice at seven a.m. Sundays we will not practice. That is a day of rest. Understood?"

"Yes, sensei!"

"I do not tolerate tardiness or disobedience. You must be as disciplined in your private life as you are in your training. Disobedience will be punished. Understood?"

"Yes, sensei!"

"Excellent. Wait here. I have something for you."

They all stood up together. The boys remained in place as Mr. Soji walked off and disappeared through the door in the back of the dojo.

He reappeared quickly, carrying clothing of some type. They were ghis, uniforms worn when taking martial arts. Mr. Soji walked up to the boys and handed one each to Connor and Wade.

"These are for you. I hope they fit."

Wade looked at Mr. Soji with awe. "Thank you, sensei Soji. This is awesome! Thank you!"

Connor was just as excited. "Yes, sir, thank you!"

"It is my pleasure. Now, we will meet back here tomorrow, same time, in uniform. Until then…Rei!"

The three boys came to attention and bowed towards their sensei, who returned the bow. "Good night, Connor and Wade. Nick, I will see you at home."

"Yes, sir!"

They turned to walk out, putting their shoes back on before doing so.

After they exited the dojo Nick turned to his buddies. "So? What didja think?"

"Aw, dude! This is gonna be frickin' awesome! I can't wait to start actually training!" Wade was hyped up.

Connor was equally upbeat. "Oh, man! Your dad is ultimately cool! I mean, giving us uniforms, and not charging us for the lessons? Wow!"

Nick was a little more subdued. "Well, what one is given, much is expected in return. My dad expects a lot out of you…out of *us*. So let's do this, yes?"

"Yes. Absolutely. We won't let your dad down." Connor was still admiring his ghi.

"Yeah, dude. We're a team. We do this together."

"Alright. Ready for the run home?"

"Let's hit it, ninja master!" Wade was getting more in to this as the days went by.

"Off we go then!"

With that the three boys took off running.

Chapter XIX: Meditate…

The next day Connor, Wade, and Nick met after school. After changing into running clothes they had brought from home they ran straight to the dojo, which was about a mile away. They removed their shoes and walked in, heading immediately to the bathrooms to change into their ghis.

After they changed Nick led them in their warm-ups. As they finished up their exercises Mr. Soji appeared. Nick walked over to the edge of the mat and Connor and Wade followed. They took their positions on the floor in front of their sensei.

The three boys bowed (Nick and Connor had been practicing), waiting for sensei Soji to return the bow before returning to an upright position.

"Sit, please." They took their places on the mat. "Before we begin, tell me: what do you think is the most important thing you must do when engaged in a fight?"

Wade answered first. "I would think that, maybe, you should make sure you have a proper stance?"

"That is a good guess. Connor?"

"Hmmm. Keep from getting hit."

"Not such a good guess. No. Nick, what is the most important thing to remember when you find yourself in a fight?"

"Most important is to relax. You must remain calm and not allow your emotions to overpower you. If you do you lose focus. If you lose focus you make mistakes. If you make mistakes you are defeated."

“Very good. Relax. Focus. Remain calm. When you get tense, when you begin to allow emotion to overcome you, focus is lost and your training goes out the window. At that point you are nothing more than a street brawler, and you will, most likely, lose.

“So, today we will begin with meditation. Not the yoga-type stuff you see today with incense and gooey fluffy music, but we are going to relax and calm our minds. Through meditation we learn to relax our minds, free our minds from unnecessary thought. A true state of meditation is one of working, doing, and being, where superficial thoughts are discarded and constructive things are taking place.”

“How will meditation help us if we’re in the middle of a fight, sensei? I mean, Zack isn’t going to just sit and wait for me to get my meditation done.”

“Connor, first I want you to forget Zack. Zack is not your concern right now. You are here, and here is where your mind must be. Zack is out there, not in here.

“Now, think of a pond, calm, serene, and undisturbed. The surface is like glass. Now we pick up a rock and throw it into the pond. Wade, what happens?”

“A splash, and ripples.”

“Correct. Then what?”

“The ripples stop and the pond reverts back to its original state. Calm and serene.”

“Correct again. The water reacts proportionately to the stone. It reacts to the weight of the stone and the force with which the stone was thrown. The response of the water is equal to the original action, no more, no less.

“Now think of a river. The river flows strong and fast. It is kept in check by and follows the river banks.

Connor, what happens if the river is swollen by rain and overcomes the riverbank?"

"Well, the water runs everywhere. It floods the surrounding land."

"Yes. The water runs everywhere, and depending on how severe the flooding, wreaks havoc on surrounding towns, destroying homes, washing away crops. In short: chaos. It is very destructive, but no purpose is achieved. Keep the river within the banks and you achieve your purpose, whether it is watering crops or producing electricity.

"Meditation will allow you to achieve these two goals. Like the water in the pond you will learn to react properly to any force with equal force, no more, no less. This will allow you to achieve a productive state of mind in the face of a dangerous situation. Your actions and reactions must be proportionate to the situation at hand, just as the water in the pond.

"As with the river you will learn to channel your energy and abilities to achieve your purpose. Channel your energy as the river channels the water. Allow the water to overrun the riverbanks and it will flow aimlessly. Keep it within the riverbanks and you have a very powerful force at your disposal."

Mr. Soji allowed the lesson to sink in momentarily. "Now we will meditate. Put your hands together in your lap, like so." He put his left and right hands together and laid them in his lap, palms up. The three boys copied him.

"Good. Now, back erect, head up…very good. We will now clear our minds of all unnecessary thoughts. Focus on your breathing. I want you to breathe in through your nose and out through your mouth. Breathe deeply and slowly."

The boys were all concentrating on their breathing. Nick was used to this but for Connor and Wade it was proving difficult.

"Sensei, how do we get unnecessary thoughts out of our heads?" Connor asked.

"It is not easy, especially for someone who has never done it before. You are used to having your brain assaulted daily with music, television, noise…here there are no distractions. It is something that comes with time and practice. You will learn in time. Now, be quiet and breathe."

Connor returned to focusing on his breathing and trying to clear his head. He couldn't seem to do it, however. Thoughts kept popping into his mind; school, Zack, his parents, Zack, pizza, Zack… He shook his head as if that would toss everything out, but it didn't help.

"Connor, just relax. It will come with time."

"Yes, sensei."

Wade was having a better time of it. He was much more laid back anyway so this was not much of a stretch for him. Nick, of course, had no trouble at all.

They sat in total silence for ten minutes. "Now everyone come back to reality…open your eyes."

Mr. Soji motioned to Wade. "Wade, what were your thoughts as you meditated?"

"Well, surfing, and…well, surfing. I like the ocean. The sound of the waves relaxes me. I guess that's why I like surfing so much."

"I see. And you, Connor? What were your thoughts as you meditated?"

"I couldn't seem to shut my brain up, sensei."

"What do you mean?"

"I mean, I couldn't stop thinking about stuff. Nothing in particular. Home, school, and…Zack. Yeah, Zack kept popping into my head. I couldn't stop no matter how hard I tried. The more he popped into my head the harder it got to clear my mind."

"You must learn to quell the anger you have towards this person. You must learn to expel him from your head. He has taken up residence in your head but he is living there rent-free. You must evict him."

"I tried. But I just couldn't pull it off. Jeez! Just the thought of him and the way he…"

Mr. Soji cut him off with a wave of his hand. "Again, the art of meditation takes time to master. A lot of time. It does not just happen. You, too, will get better at it in time."

"Yes, sensei."

"You must work on your meditation much as you work on your physical well-being, your skills in the martial arts, or any other aspect of your life in which you desire to become proficient. To that end I expect you to meditate three times daily in ten-minute increments. Once when you wake in the morning, once before you go to sleep in the evening, and we will meditate here before we begin our instruction. Is that clear?"

"Yes, sensei," all three said in unison. They were getting pretty good at that.

"Good. Now it is instruction time. Come with me." He got up and headed for the back followed by the boys, taking position by the speed bag.

"This is a speed bag. It is used mainly by boxers, but also in the martial arts. It serves many purposes. It helps to develop hand-eye coordination, conditions your reflexes, and it increases arm strength and endurance. Here, Nick will show you how it is done. Nick, please." He motioned for Nick to step up.

Nick held the bag in his right hand and punched it with his left, not too hard, and then hit it again with his left. He then hit it with his right, and again with his right. He repeated this a few times slowly, and then gradually began to get faster until the bag was just a blur. The bag made a sound somewhat like someone dribbling a basketball as Nick continued to work it.

Connor and Wade were amazed at the ease with which Nick pounded away at the bag. His hands were going in tight little circles, never missing a beat.

"This will be your first task to master. Once you have mastered it we will move on. That is enough, Okita."

Nick busted out a few more rounds and finished with a solid punch at the end that echoed throughout the dojo. He stepped back from the bag, almost stepping on Wade as he did so.

Mr. Soji motioned to Connor. "Connor, you will be first. Come, come."

Connor stepped up and came face-to-face with the speed bag. He stood there for a moment, and then looked up to Mr. Soji with a "What do I do now?" look.

"First," sensei Soji said, "...make sure the bag is the proper height. It should be at chin height. It is already there so you are set.

"Next get into a proper stance. Feet shoulder width apart, shoulders square with the bag. Make sure you are close enough that you will not have to extend your arms more than a few inches, but not so close that you will get hit in the head with the rebound from the bag."

Connor put his feet shoulder width apart as he was told, faced the bag and squared his shoulders with it. He put his left arm out to check the distance, adjusting his stance accordingly.

"Now hold your fists up at chin level. Your arms should be bent at a ninety-degree angle and your upper arms should be parallel with the ground."

He put his fists up and bent his arms, ensuring they were parallel with the ground as Mr. Soji had instructed him.

"Excellent. Now begin."

Connor took the bag in his left hand, took a deep breath, and hit the bag. It hit the board and rebounded quickly. He tried to hit it again but missed.

He stopped the bag, grabbing it again, and took another shot at it. He tried to hit it again with the same result. He huffed, stopped the bag and took it in his hand again.

"Connor, do not allow yourself to get frustrated. This is your first time doing this. It is something that takes practice, but it also takes patience. Control your anger, control your emotions. You must do this above all else."

"Yes, sensei." He took a deep breath and hit the bag, not as hard as before. This time he was able to connect on the second hit, but missed when he went to switch hands.

"Continue to practice, all of you. Okita, I expect you to work with them. Understood?"

"Yes, sensei."

"Good. I have something to attend to. Continue to practice. I will be back shortly."

Sensei Soji walked away, disappearing into an office off to the side as the boys continued their practice with the speed bag.

****

After an hour Mr. Soji returned. Wade was at the bag and doing quite well. Not super, but well enough for a beginner. As he approached the boys stopped, faced their sensei, and bowed.

"Very good, Wade. You seem to be a natural for it."

"Well, it was a rocky start, but a little practice and it just kind of started working. It's not difficult once you get a rhythm."

"How about you, Connor? Show me what you can do."

"Yes, sir."

He stepped up to the bag and took his stance. He began punching with his right hand and got a couple of hits in before he flubbed it. He stopped, stepped back and took a deep breath.

Stepping up again he took his stance and started over. A little more careful this time, he was able to keep it going. Not as fast as Wade, but at least he got the basic concept down.

"Very good, Connor. You need much practice, but you will do fine. Come, let's wrap up our session for today."

The boys all faced their sensei. "Do not forget, tonight before you sleep you must meditate. When you wake up tomorrow you must meditate. Do not be discouraged if you cannot quiet your mind. Try your best. It will come with time.

"You have all done very well today. We will see you tomorrow then.

The boys bowed in unison, which sensei Soji returned. "Good night, boys."

"Thank you, sensei." Connor was especially thankful for the opportunity given them by Nick's dad.

After changing and retrieving their shoes they began their run home. The sun was bright, the weather was warm but not too warm, and the day seemed, to Connor, somehow sweeter. Things were looking up.

Chapter XX: Never Walk Alone

The lessons were going well for Connor and Wade. They had both gotten proficient at the speed bag over the course of one week and were now working on the punching bag as well. They both felt their confidence levels rising as they got better and were looking forward to beginning lessons with actual martial arts.

Connor, Wade, and Nick had taken to walking to school together after their morning run and exercises. Today, however, Wade had a doctor's appointment in the early morning and Nick had a dental appointment, so Connor was left to walk to school alone. He thought nothing of it as he left his house at the usual time.

Ordinarily the three boys took the regular route to school and didn't worry about running into Zack. There was strength in numbers, after all, and Zack was surely loathe to tangle with Nick again. This morning, however, Connor didn't give a thought to the fact that he was alone. That left him vulnerable…extremely vulnerable.

It was a gorgeous spring morning. The sun was just beginning to warm things up though it was still a bit chilly. He was about two blocks from the school thinking about practice that afternoon and what the lesson would entail.

He never saw it coming.

The force with which he was jerked back almost took him out of his shoes. "What the…?!?"

He didn't finish the thought as he was lifted up and tossed on the ground next to the sidewalk. He landed with a muffled thud as he hit the grass. Totally disoriented he was slow to recover as a second attack was unleashed from his unseen assailant, this time in the form of a kick to the ribs.

The force of the kick sent him rolling. As he rolled over he caught a glimpse of his assailant…Zack.

“Not so tough without your little friends around, are you, worm?” He emphasized the word “worm” with another kick to the gut. “I’ll teach you to make a punk out of me.”

Connor tried to get up but he was in extreme pain, and Zack was relentless. As he tried to get to one knee Zack pushed him back down and straddled his back.

Connor was helpless. Zack was much heavier than he was and in his current position he could not get up nor could he move.

Zack grabbed Connor’s hair and pulled his head back, like a rider on horseback pulling the reins of his steed. He put his face right next to Connor’s, allowing Connor to get a whiff of the awful stink of his breath.

“Listen to me, you little piss-ant. Are you listening?”

Connor didn’t respond.

“I SAID…ARE…YOU…LISTENING…YOU LITTLE WORM!” He slammed Connor’s head into the ground and rubbed his face in the grass, then pulled his head back again, this time with more force.

Connor's voice came out as a hoarse whisper: “Piss off, jackass.”

Zack slammed his head into the ground again, and then backhanded him for good measure. He pulled

Connor's head back yet again, putting his mouth right next to Connor's ear.

His voice dripped with contempt and hatred. "I don't know who you think you are, worm, but I can promise you this: you are a marked man. Anytime I catch you, or your little blond-haired surfer boyfriend, or both of you together, you take what happened to you here today and multiply it by ten. I'm through dicking around with you. I'm through with your little tough-guy act.

"Anytime I catch you alone you're mine. And I'll be watching, don't doubt that, worm. I've got my eye on you, and I'm keeping track.

"Screw with me again, you little panty-stain. I'll beat you so bad your parents will need dental records to identify you, if they can find your teeth. You got me?"

Connor started to say something, but nothing came out. Just a strained groan as he tried to breathe.

"Don't forget…I'll be watching you."

Zack pushed his head into the ground, hard, and then punched the back of his head for good measure. He got up, started to turn to walk away, and then thought better of it, instead giving Connor one more stiff kick in his thigh. Satisfied he had made his point he walked off, looking around to make sure nobody had seen the attack.

Zack looked over his shoulder as he walked away. "I'll be seeing you, worm." He waved and then turned around for good.

****

Connor lay on the ground, bloody nose, his forehead bleeding profusely from two gashes, his ribs and his gut throbbing with pain. He was certain he had a broken rib or two, the pain was so intense.

He tried to get up, tried to get to his knees but his body wouldn't let him. So he lay there for a few minutes more.

He was breathing heavily and began to feel himself begin to inhale in heaves. The tears wanted to flow but he willed them back. He would not cry. He refused to cry.

He tried to get up again, this time succeeding in getting to one knee. His ribs hurt something fierce, and now he noticed his leg was hurting as well. His face was filthy from being shoved into the ground repeatedly. He could feel the warm stickiness of the blood running around his lips and down his chin. Had he knocked a tooth out or something? He checked his teeth…nope, all there, all in place. He was certain nothing was broken.

Anger welled up inside him as before, but what could he do? Zack was gone. He could punch the fence that was there, but to what avail? He'd probably break his hand. At least he had control enough of his emotions to keep from doing something that stupid and pointless.

He stood up slowly, looked around to see if anyone else was around, someone who might have seen him get the snot beat out of him.

Nobody. Good.

He brushed himself off as best as he could, but he was filthy and covered in blood. His face was bloody, his neck was blood-streaked, his shirt was bloody, and his pants and shirt were filthy. No way was he going to school looking like this.

He stood for a moment, not quite sure what to do. The urge to let loose with the tears had been successfully defeated but the anger was still there and getting more intense by the second.

He struggled to contain his rage. He knew that it would be pointless to let his anger out, but it was overwhelming him!

He sat down in the grass and put his head on his knees, hands on the back of his head. He began to breathe as deeply as he could. After about five minutes he had quelled the feelings of rage enough he was able to think a bit more clearly.

Where to from here? He checked his watch: it was almost eight o'clock. His dad would have already left for work, and his mom would be leaving shortly to run errands and do some shopping, she had said that morning. Maybe she was already gone.

Connor decided he would head home, clean up, and change into some clean clothes and then head back to school. He would have to make up an excuse for being late but that was no big deal. School began at quarter after eight, so he could get home and change in time to get back to school by eight-thirty.

Done.

He headed for home, limping badly, hoping his mom had already left for the day.

****

As he approached his house Connor saw that both vehicles were gone. Good. He could get in, get changed, and get to school.

He went around back and entered through the garage. He headed straight to his room to change.

Should he take another shower? He smelled his pits (nobody could see him anyways) and decided he just needed to wash his face and hands, maybe his arms.

He didn't realize how much blood had made its way to his shirt until he took it off. Crap. He couldn't very well let his mom see *that* now, could he?

He took his shirt and went to the garage where they kept their trash can. He opened the lid and took out one of the already tied-up bags. It took a little work but he was able to get the bag untied. He threw his shirt in the bag, re-tied it and put it back in the trash can. Hopefully his mom wouldn't miss it.

He went back to his room and finished undressing. After reassessing his condition he decided a quick shower was in order after all. There was blood everywhere, and his hair was matted with blood and sweat.

As he walked towards the shower he got his first glimpse of himself in the mirror. Holy crap…he looked in the mirror and he didn't like what he saw looking back. It looked like something out of a horror movie.

The blood had coagulated on his face giving him a grotesque appearance. He looked like an emergency room trauma victim.

That didn't concern him, though. What really concerned him was the black eye he was now aware of, as well as the abrasion on his forehead that was bleeding slightly.

Studying his body more he checked his ribs, which he could now see were bruised badly. It was mostly red now but he was certain it would turn purple and green later. He definitely couldn't let his folks see that. They were going to see the black eye, however, as well as the head abrasion. Well, he could talk his way around that:

What, dad? Oh, I got hit at karate practice. Yep, Wade threw an elbow and popped me in the eye. Yeah, he's so clumsy! The abrasion? Well, when he hit me with the elbow I fell and scraped my head against the carpet. Yes, we have a mat, but I was right at the edge and darn if I didn't fall onto the carpet! No, dad, I'm fine, really.

Yeah, right. Maybe it would work, maybe not. Even if his dad bought it, Mrs. Lundy had an uncanny ability to ferret out information, and if she was even the slightest bit suspicious of his story, game over, dude. That woman should have been in the FBI. She'd have criminals singing within two minutes. She was that good.

Connor hated lying to his parents, but if he told them what really happened there would be a big to-do about it, conference with the principal, the teacher, an attempt to talk to Zack's parents, and Zack himself.

No, Connor told himself. Lying in this instance was justified. The alternative was much worse: more attention from Zack and a more hellish existence than the one he was living now. If that came to pass Zack would be relentless in his tormenting. He was going to have to practice his story a few times to make it sound convincing.

He came back to reality as he noticed the time on the clock. He had dawdled long enough. He jumped in the shower and washed as quickly as he could.

He dried off quickly. He then gave himself a once-over in the mirror, making sure he had gotten all of the blood off. "Good grief," he thought as he looked at the damage. How was he going to explain these injuries?

He walked back to his room and put on a new shirt. Looking at the clock he saw it was eight-twenty. Crap. If he hustled he could get to class by eight-thirty, but with a limp he was looking at eight-forty more realistically.

He left his room and stopped in the hall bathroom to check himself out once more before leaving. Satisfied he had done all he could to make himself presentable he left the house, locking the door behind him, and ran to school. Well, more half-jogged, half-limped to school, but it was the best he could do.

****

It was a quarter ‘till nine when Connor got to school. He walked into class, handed Mrs. Barber his note, and went directly to his seat. He avoided the stares of his classmates and their urgent whispers as they were undoubtedly discussing their theories about his latest incident amongst themselves. Again.

Mrs. Barber looked at the note, looked at Connor over her glasses, then back at the note. She put the note on her desk, considered Connor for a moment, and thankfully didn’t ask any questions.

Connor opened a book (it didn't matter which one) and stared at it. He would occasionally flip a page but he wasn't fooling anybody. He didn't care. He just immersed himself in his own cocoon, becoming increasingly oblivious to everyone and everything around him.

The end-of-class bell jarred him back to reality. He slammed his book shut, jammed it into his book bag and took off like a shot for his next class. He exited the room and turned right.

The crush of students in the hall trying to get to class was suffocating, but he was unconcerned. He rounded the corner, a few doors from his class when he looked up and saw him. Connor froze in his tracks allowing the throng of students to jostle him around as they made their way to their classes.

Connor's eyes caught Zack's. A flash of recognition washed over Zack's face, and he grinned that evil, crap-eating grin Connor knew all too well.

Zack stared at him, then brought his hand up to his throat and drew his finger across it from one side to the other. Zack then put his fingers to his eyes and pointed them back towards Connor. "I'm watching you…" was the message he was conveying, and Connor got it.

He pressed on to class, which was a couple of doors before he would have passed Zack. He ducked into his class and quickly sat in the far corner of the room where he couldn't be seen from the hall.

The class began to fill quickly, but Connor didn't acknowledge anybody. He had pulled out another book and just stared into it.

He wasn't sure if he was embarrassed, angry, or really, truly scared. Zack had done a number on him this morning. His confidence had been shaken, and shaken badly. The bravado that he normally brought to the fore when confronted with bullies like Zack was gone. It had shriveled up and hid somewhere in the deep, dark crevices of his psyche, and he wasn't sure if he wanted to find it.

Where the hell was Wade?

Chapter XXI: The Point Of It All

It was lunch time and Wade still hadn't shown up. Maybe his mom took him home, or maybe the doctor was a psycho who used him in an experiment where a weasel was grafted onto his head. Right. Get a grip, Connor told himself.

He didn't feel like going to the lunch room to eat opting instead to head out to the big tree in the back of the school yard he and Wade frequented. He knew he would have to endure the stares of his classmates and the same questions over and over and over and over. He had already been the subject of an inquiry from many of his classmates, all of which he ignored completely.

Connor sat under the tree, enjoying the shade and the breeze. He leaned his head back and shut his eyes listening to the cacophony of voices and squeals coming from the jumble of students milling about the school yard. He was relaxed for the first time today and thought he could just fall asleep right here if he were so inclined.

The relaxation was short-lived, however, as the memory of the day's events began to slowly creep back into his mind. He tried to cast them out of his head but they kept on coming and would not stop. The more the thoughts assaulted his mind the angrier he became.

It wasn't right, he thought. It wasn't right that he had to endure Zack's torment. It wasn't right that Zack could walk around with impunity terrorizing anyone he decided needed terrorizing. It wasn't right that he, and many others, had to watch their backs at all times lest they become Zack's latest shake-down target. No, it wasn't right.

He was sitting upright now, staring out at the school yard. He scanned the sea of faces looking for one in particular, but his best friend was nowhere to be found.

A feeling of apprehension came over him suddenly and he started scanning the immediate area around him. He looked all over and even up in the tree as if Zack were hanging there just waiting to descend from above to deliver another thrashing, this time in front of everyone in the school.

It turned out to be a case of paranoia on Connor's part. "Great," Connor said silently to himself, "…now I'm getting paranoid. Just frickin' great." He gave the area another quick scan, just in case, but Zack was nowhere to be seen.

The bell rang signifying the end of the lunch period. He sat under the tree silently, seething with anger. He noticed his hands were now clenched fists. He unclenched them and tried to tame his thoughts, but to no avail.

He remained under the tree until the last student had entered the school. The bell rang to begin the next class but still he did not move from his spot. He remained there for a full ten minutes.

He was alone outside, everyone else having gone in to get to class. Finally he got up but he did not head into the school. He instead began walking in the opposite direction, away from the school and off the school grounds.

He wasn't sure where he was going, figuring he would know where he was going when he got there.

****

Connor dawdled for awhile, not really sure what to do. He was certainly going to get in trouble for leaving school but at this particular moment he didn't much care. He would deal with that when it became necessary.

Maybe he could be home-schooled. That would be cool, wouldn't it? Not having to go to school, not worrying about who you're going to run into…

On second thought, nah. His mom wouldn't go for that. For the moment this was his lot in life. He just had to deal with it.

He could not go home, that was certain. Neither could he go to Wade's house. He came to realize he couldn't go anywhere near his neighborhood lest he be spotted by someone he knows, or worse, his parents. Not only that, but Zack knew he was alone today and may be waiting for him again. Would he attack Connor twice in one day?

Of course he would. The jerk had no honor, no sense of decency. He wouldn't hesitate to attack again if given the chance. He was evil incarnate.

No, going anywhere near his neighborhood was out of the question. He continued his aimless wander.

Twenty minutes later Connor found himself at the dojo. It was a nondescript spot, a strip mall on a two-lane road. The dojo itself was wedged in between a hair salon and an appliance repair shop, though it took up two store fronts.

He stood outside for a moment, hesitating before deciding whether or not to walk in. Sensei Soji's car was parked out front so he was surely inside, but what would he say about Connor being out of school?

Where else was he going to go? Besides, he had to be here in a few hours anyway for practice. Maybe sensei would allow him to hang around, maybe get in a light workout before this afternoon's lesson.

He grabbed the door handle, paused, then pulled the door open and walked in. He removed his shoes upon entering and bowed before stepping onto the mat.

He was about to head towards the speed bag when sensei Soji appeared. "Ah, Connor. Hello, hello."

Connor turned towards Mr. Soji and bowed, which his sensei returned. "Hi, sensei Soji."

"What are you doing here so early? Why are you not in school?" Mr. Soji at first could not see the injuries on Connor's face which was silhouetted by the glare from the windows at the storefront.

"I, uh…it's a long story, sensei."

"I see." Then he really did see…he saw the black eye and the gash on Connor's forehead that Zack was kind enough to give him.

"Connor! What happened to you? Where did you get that?"

Connor had to chuckle. Where did he get that, as if it was something he could order off Ebay or pick up at the local mall. He squelched the urge to give a witty retort. He didn't want to anger Mr. Soji, not after all he had done for him.

"That's not all, sensei." He lifted his shirt to reveal the injury to his ribs. The area had already begun to turn purple and green, and covered his side from his armpit down to his midsection. “My leg’s pretty messed up, too.”

“Come, come. Sit with me and tell me what happened.” Mr. Soji motioned for Connor to follow him. He walked to the center of the mat and sat down. Connor sat down opposite him.

Sensei Soji could see Connor’s face much better now. The cut on his forhead was not that bad but his eye looked awful. “Now, tell me what has happened.”

Connor didn’t know where to begin. He took a deep breath, and then another.

“I tell you what. Stop. Let us meditate first. Come. Meditate.”

“Yes, sensei.” How could he meditate at a time like this? Well, no sense fighting it.

Connor folded his hands in his lap and closed his eyes. He tried to clear his mind, but as before it was no use, and now it was just that much harder given the day’s events. The pain rippling through his body did not help matters.

“You must learn to clear your mind, Connor. Relax, let everything go, free your mind from its burdens.”

“It is hard, sensei. Today has been difficult.”

“It should matter not how difficult your day has been. The events of the day are inconsequential. You must train your mind to let go, to empty your mind of its burdens.”

Connor tried but could not get the images of Zack pounding his head into the ground out of his mind. He concentrated on his breathing, in through the nose, out through the mouth, but still the images persisted.

"I'm in a lot of pain, sensei. It makes it difficult to focus."

"Forget about the pain. Ignore it. It is there. There is nothing you can do about it. Work through the pain. Focus your mind."

"Yes, sensei."

They sat in silence for about ten minutes. Sensei Soji clapped his hands together signaling the end of the meditation session.

“Do not be distressed that you cannot clear your mind. As I said before, it will take much time before you learn to meditate properly. Now, tell me what happened today. And please, leave out no details.”

Connor proceeded to relay everything that had happened that morning. It didn’t take long.

****

“…and then I just left. I didn’t want to go back to class ‘cause I was tired of everyone staring, giggling, asking questions. I sat outside for a few minutes after the bell rang, and after everyone else had gone inside I just got up and left. I don’t know what came over me. I just know I didn’t want to be there any more.

“I didn’t have a plan, but I knew I couldn’t go home. I just kind of wandered a bit and found myself here. So, here I am.”

“And what did you expect when you got here?”

“I don’t know. Like I said, I didn’t plan to be here. But when I got here I was thinking maybe I could just work out until time for lessons or something. Would that be alright with you?” He looked hopeful.

Mr. Soji considered his student for a moment before speaking. “There will be times, Connor, when you must face difficult situations. If you cannot withstand simple comments from your classmates how will you withstand the bully who looks to harm you? Comments are mere words.

“When your classmates say these things they are looking to get a reaction out of you. If you give them the reaction they are looking for they will continue to make more comments hoping to get a bigger reaction out of you. They are pushing your buttons.

“Sure, some of them are just looking for a story to tell at your expense, but you must not let them get to you. You cannot run away. And that is what you have done today. You have run away.

“A fight is not won by one punch or one kick. Either learn to endure or hire a body guard.”

Connor let that one sink in.

“Well, I can’t afford a body guard, so I guess I better learn to endure.”

“Yes, you must learn to endure, and that includes the endless stares and crude comments of your classmates. Nobody can make you feel inferior without your consent, Connor. You did nothing wrong, and you had no chance to fight back.

“Hold your head high. Greet the comments and stares with a smile. Nobody expects that. They expect you to cry, to whine, to pity yourself. They want you to indulge their morbid curiosity. Don't give in to it. The stares and comments will stop when they see that it doesn't bother you. You will be the better person for it. Agreed?"

"Yes, sensei."

"Now, we need to get you back to school."

"How? My parents have no idea I'm out and…"

"Do not worry about that. I will drive you back to school, and then I will talk to Mr. Greevy, the principal."

"You're not my dad, so you can't sign me in, Mr. Soji."

"Mr. Greevy happens to be one of my assistants here. He is quite good, though he has much to learn. I'm sure he'll understand. And then, when the school day actually ends, come back for your lesson. I think we need to change your training regimen, starting today."

Mr. Soji moved to get up and Connor followed suit, getting to his feet before his sensei. As Mr. Soji stood Connor bowed.

"Come, let's get you back to school."

****

Mr. Soji drove Connor back to school from the dojo. Upon arriving he spoke with the principal, Mr. Greevy, explaining the situation to him while Connor sat in the waiting area.

Mr. Soji came out of the principal's office with Mr. Greevy after a few minutes, both of them laughing as if they had been sharing jokes.

How the heck could they be joking at a time like this, Connor thought? He stood up as they walked out of the office and slowly walked towards them.

"Well, sensei Soji, thank you for bringing him back. I'll take care of everything." Mr. Greevy looked down at Connor and took note of his facial injuries. "Yeah, you got it pretty good, didn't you?"

"Yes, sir. I suppose so." The embarrassment began to creep back into his mind again, but he remembered what sensei Soji had said earlier: 'No one can make you feel inferior without your consent.' With that he pushed it back down and managed a half-hearted smile as he tried to play it off.

"Better luck next time, I guess," Connor said.

"I will see you this afternoon. Nick's mother dropped him off just after lunch so wait for him after school so you two can run to practice together. O.K.?"

"Will do, Mr. Soji. Um, thanks for setting me straight. And for getting me back to school. And for talking with Mr. Greevy."

"You are most welcome." He smiled at Connor, and then looked up to Mr. Greevy. "Thank you again, Bill." He turned and walked out.

Mr. Greevy turned to Connor. "Well, looks like you've had quite a day, Mr. Lundy. Don't worry about anything. I can't say I would have done anything differently were I in your shoes. But in the future if you get the hankerin' to leave campus, or if you are having a problem with something, please come see me first, O.K.?"

"Yes, sir. Thank you." It was good to know he had someone to turn to if need be.

"Good! Now that we have that squared away, here's your pass. Now get to class."

"Yes, sir." Connor took the note. "Thanks again, Mr. Greevy."

He turned and walked out of the office and headed to class.

****

Connor was supposed to be in biology at present. He stopped off at his locker to retrieve his books then headed to the classroom. He walked into the class where Ms. Benitez was lecturing at the white board.

He stood at the doorway until she had finished her point at which time she motioned him over. He ignored the stares of his classmates as he walked over to her. His limp had mostly disappeared as he tried to walk straight and ignore the pain in his thigh. He was mostly successful.

Wade was at his desk having been dropped off by his mom after his doctor appointment. He was shocked when he saw the condition his best friend was in.

Connor handed the note to Ms. Benitez. As she began to scan the note he proceeded to his desk. He took out his books and looked over at a classmate to figure out where to turn in the book.

Ms. Benitez finished the note. She looked up, giving Connor a cursory glance before setting the note on her desk and continuing the lesson.

Connor never looked over to his friend. Wade would have to wait.

The bell rang ten minutes later. The class moved as one as everyone jumped at the sound. Everyone except Connor, who sat in his desk until most other students had filed out of the classroom. He calmly closed his book, picked up his things, and headed for the door.

Ms. Benitez looked up as he passed her desk.

"Connor?"

Connor stopped at her desk. "Yes, ma'am?"

"Connor, is everything alright? I mean, are you O.K.? What's going on?"

"I'm fine, Ms. Benitez. Really. I'll be fine. Thank you for asking, though."

"Connor…"

"Really, Ms. Benitez, I'll be alright. Thanks." He offered her a smile as he turned to leave. Ms. Benitez watched as he exited the classroom, shrugged her shoulders, and then turned her attention to the lesson for the incoming class.

As Connor expected Wade was hanging out in the hallway waiting for him to come out.

"What's up?"

"What's up? You're AWOL last class, then you show up late to this class with a whopper of a shiner and a head wound, and you're asking me what's up?"

"Well, what do you want me to say? It's pretty obvious what happened, and I'm sure I don't need to explain it to you in graphic detail. Zack jumped me this morning."

"He jumped you?"

"Ambushed is more like it. I never saw him, never heard him. One second I'm walking, the next I'm flying. He jumped me, end of story."

They arrived at their lockers (Connor's locker was two doors down from Wade's) and proceeded to retrieve their books for the next class.

"So, you were by yourself?"

"Yes, I was by myself! What do you think? You had a doctor's appointment, Nick had a dental appointment. I wasn't thinking and walked to school by myself, and I used the main route to school. Stupid me. I know."

"Dang, dude. Well, it could have been worse, I suppose."

"It is worse." He lifted his shirt to reveal the bruising on his side. "See? It is worse."

"Holy crap! Hey, man…"

"Don't worry about it. I'll be fine."

They finished collecting their books, slammed their lockers shut and headed off to their next class, English with Mr. Richardson. Connor could feel the eyes of people in the hall as he made his way through the throng, or so he thought.

"So, where were you after lunch?"

"I left."

"You left…where? Your folks pick you up?"

"No, I just left. I was sitting under the tree at lunch and I didn't feel like going to class. So I left."

"Dude! You can't just leave campus, man! Did you get in trouble? How'd you get back?"

"I ended up at the dojo, and Mr. Soji was there, so I went in. I was hoping maybe he'd let me hang out before lessons today, but we talked things over and he brought me back to school. He smoothed things over with Mr. Greevy."

"Wow. Lucky you."

"Yeah. Turns out Mr. Greevy is an assistant instructor at the dojo two nights a week."

"I swear, dude, I can't leave you alone for five minutes!"

They arrived at Mr. Richardson's class. "Look, man. Don't talk about this with anyone, alright? I'll be fine, really."

"You don't have to worry about me. I am a lock-box." He put his hand to his mouth and turned it as one would turn a key. "Gone, dude. But, uh, what are you gonna tell your folks? It's not like they aren't gonna notice that."

"I'm working on it. I'll just tell 'em I had a little accident at practice, or something."

"Swell. You gonna be able to run today?"

"I have a bruised eye, not a broken leg, doofus." He didn't bother to mention the injury to his thigh.

"Alright, alright. Just checking, ding-dong. Don't get all testy."

Connor managed a grin. "I know."

They walked into the classroom, eager for the day to be over.

Chapter XXII: Serious Training

The boys met up after school to head to the dojo as they did each day. They were delayed a bit as Connor filled Nick in on the happenings of the day.

Clouds had rolled in during the afternoon casting the sky a deep gray. The three made haste to the dojo so as not to get caught in the deluge which was surely on its way.

They arrived, shedding their footwear at the front door as always, bowing as they entered. They proceeded to warm up and stretch as they awaited the arrival of sensei Soji, who entered about four minutes later.

After meditation sensei Soji had them stand up as he addressed them.

"Today we begin training in earnest. Connor, Wade; you have both come along well these past few weeks. I know you have been eager to get on with the 'real' training, but I assure you that all of the tedious, repetitive, mundane exercises have been necessary.

"So to begin, let's have some basic understandings. You have all seen martial arts movies, I'm sure, yes?"

They all nodded.

"Well, forget about anything you've seen in a movie. It's all Hollywood. Most of it is made up, and the stuff that isn't made up is executed poorly. The only exception would be a Bruce Lee film, and even then Master Bruce took some liberties because, as he said, it made it look better for the audience. Therefore you will put out of your mush-filled skulls any moves or techniques you may have seen in a Hollywood movie.

"From here on out Nick will be my assistant, helping you with your moves, techniques, and such. He is not your sensei, just my assistant. Understand?"

"Yes, sensei."

"Good. Okita, if you would, please..." Mr. Soji motioned for Nick to come to his side.

"We will start simple, of course, and once you have mastered a skill we will move on to the next. Only when you have mastered the skill will we move on.

"Now, there are some basic tenets that you must learn and understand. First: when you are engaged in a fight you must know when to move and when to not move. In other words, you must move when you choose, only when necessary. You must conserve your movements, remain calm. In truth you are moving just before it is necessary, being flexible to adapt to the changing circumstances.

"You must be fluid, not tense, not rigid. As we discussed earlier, be like the water, adapting to whatever crosses your path. If it moves in front of you, move around it. If it opens up, fill it.

"You must take advantage of every situation. When an opportunity presents itself, take it. Do not hesitate, for hesitation will surely lead to defeat. When an opening presents itself put everything into it as soon as it opens."

Connor and Wade listened with rapt attention. They were utterly fascinated by the lesson (this was the meat of it after all, and what they had been waiting for all along) and thankful to be there. They took in every word.

Sensei Soji continued. “Third, never, ever do the same thing twice. Be unpredictable. This is not to say that you are haphazard. Quite the contrary. You always have a plan, but do not fall into a pattern. This we will discuss as it applies to what happened this morning with Connor."

Connor's face turned a light shade of crimson at the mention of his "incident." Whether it was from embarrassment or anger he was unsure. A bit of both, probably.

Mr. Soji continued: “Finally, be confident. At all times be confident, never doubting for an instant that you are in control of the situation and that you are able to overcome your adversary. Be confident in your abilities; be confident in your skills; above all be confident in yourself. If you lose confidence in these things then you are lost.”

He paused, allowing the lesson to sink in. “Do you have any questions so far?”

Connor shook his head. “No, sir. Not so far.”

“Me, either. I’m good, sensei.”

“Good. Then we can continue. Okita, stand please.”

Nick stood up and took a spot next to his dad.

“A good martial artist is always ready for anything. They are aware of their surroundings and have evaluated any and all threats. They are prepared for whatever comes their way.”

Connor got a quizzical look on his face.

“Yes, Connor? You have a question?”

"So you are saying that we need to be prepared for anything, no matter what? That seems like a lot, depending on the situation."

"In time, Connor, you will come to see that it is not so hard as you may think. If you want proficiency in anything you must practice. We will practice, and you will become proficient, provided you do what is asked of you and give one hundred percent to learning."

"I understand. Thank you, sensei."

"Now, before one steps into the fray, one is aware of their surroundings. Connor: this morning, on your way to school, you were ambushed by Zack, yes?"

Connor's face flushed again. He could feel his fists clenching by his sides. "Yes, sir. He did."

"I do not point this out to embarrass you, but to make a point. When you left your house this morning, what were you thinking?"

"Huh?"

"What were you thinking about? What was going through your mind?"

"Gee, Mr. Soji, I really don't remember. I'm just not sure."

"O.K. then, more important: what were you *not* thinking?"

Connor considered the question, wondering what the point was, figuring it out quickly. "I wasn't thinking about getting jumped, that's for sure."

"Exactly! And because this was not in your thoughts, this led to…what?"

Connor was stumped. "Getting jumped? Getting ambushed?"

"Yes, but that is not the answer I was seeking. It led to complacency; complacency in your routine. You did not assess your situation, did not evaluate the threat. You knew Zack was a threat, a danger, yet you did nothing to deter the attack. You were complacent and therefore blind to the dangers that awaited you."

Connor began to understand what sensei was talking about. "So I should have been anticipating that Zack may have been planning to ambush me?"

"Yes. You were alone this morning and you took the same route to school that you always take. You did not consider that Zack was just waiting for an opportune moment in which to attack you. And he has already warned you that he'll be watching for another moment, yes?"

"Yes." That gave Connor something to think about.

"Good. He has already exposed his plan. Use this to your advantage.

"Next, remember that anger is counter-productive. Anger only serves to reduce your efficiency. Anger leads to mistakes, and ultimately to your defeat.

"When one allows anger to overtake them then rules are disregarded, one becomes desperate, and inevitably you will do something you will regret. Everything you have learned will be forgotten. Execution of movement will suffer. You will lose. Always, always, keep a lid on your emotions."

The boys nodded as if hypnotized, but they were paying attention, not allowing anything to pass them by without being logged in to their memories.

"When engaged in combat, never telegraph your moves. Plan your moves but do not give them away.

Surprise is one of the most potent weapons in your arsenal.

"In that same vein of thought, when you find yourself faced with a situation where combat becomes inevitable, then you feign inferiority. This will encourage your attacker into believing they have a superior position and will feed into their arrogance, leading to over-confidence on their part. Allow them to believe you are inferior, lead them in, and then just when they think you are finished…you strike!

"This will surprise them, and possibly anger them. You must continue to strike while they are surprised, confused, and unsure of what has just hit them.

"Do you have any questions?"

Connor and Wade looked at one another, then back to their sensei.

"No, sir, not at the moment."

"Good. Each day, after meditation, but before going into technique we will have a class session such as this. Skills are important, but you must have the knowledge to go with those skills if you are to be effective in your discipline.

"Now let's stand up and get to work on your stance."

The rest of the class was spent working on their stances, with more to come later.

****

It was early evening as the three boys arrived in front of Connor's house. There was a breeze blowing which helped to dry the sweat that had formed on their bodies as a result of their run back after class. They were hanging out in the driveway just talking.

"Man, you really got the worst of it, didn't you?" Nick shook his head in sympathy. "I feel bad that I wasn't there."

"It happens. No worries. Nobody's fault but mine for not thinking. At least it's almost time for summer break."

"Yeah, dude. Glorious, glorious summer! Surf's up!" Wade made a "hang ten" sign with his hand as he envisioned himself hitting the waves a lot more often in the coming months.

Nick chuckled. "You won't have too much time for that this summer, I think."

"Huh? Why not?"

"We have a lot of training and studying to do over the summer. When school's out it will be the perfect time to get more proficient and improve our physical stamina. No worries about homework and school, and dad said we can come to the dojo anytime we wish, so we can do lessons earlier in the day."

"Huh. Well, there'll be some time left for surfing, won't there?"

"Oh, yeah, sure. We're gonna take breaks. I mean we don't want to overwork ourselves. We'll pace it and get a nice routine going. There'll be plenty of time for hanging out. Besides, I was hoping you could teach me how to surf, dude."

"Absolutely, little dude!"

"Sweet. Well, I gotta get inside. Homework doth beckon. See you in the morning!"

Nick turned and headed to his house.

Connor and Wade lingered for a bit.

"Well, summer is coming. If we can avoid Zack for the next few weeks I think we can relax a bit over the summer." Connor scratched the back of his neck. "Maybe he won't get promoted, again, and he'll stay in middle school while we go to Leonard High."

"Maybe, but don't count on it. Remember what Mr. Soji said: be aware of your surroundings, and always expect the unexpected."

"Yeah, you're right. I won't be making that mistake again." Connor touched his hand to his bruised eye. "Today was rough, but the pain was an afterthought after awhile."

"Yeah, but that's gonna hurt like a fool in the morning, dude. Trust me. I've had my share of injuries from surfing. It's always worse the next day."

"Well, whatever. I can handle it. Anyway, I gotta go. See you in the A.M."

"Toodles, dude." Wade gave him the "hang ten" sign again before turning and heading home.

Now Connor had to get his story straight before he faced his parents. He turned, walked up to the front door, took a deep breath, and turned the handle.

Chapter XXIII: The Learning Curve

The next day's lesson was focused on proper movement. This entailed proper stance as learned previously, except now movements were incorporated. Sensei Soji taught them how to turn properly, how to maintain balance, and proper breathing technique. Breathing, it appeared, was a huge part of doing everything right.

Mr. Soji was working with Connor while Nick worked with Wade. They were doing alright, but it was definitely going to take some time.

Nick was being patient with Wade who was taking a bit longer to get the move down that they were working on. "Not like that, like this." Nick demonstrated again. "Now, you try it."

Wade copied Nick's movement but still didn't get it quite right. "Crap! I'm never gonna get this."

Sensei Soji heard Wade's frustration and stopped for a moment, turning his way. "Wade, you must be patient. Rome was not built in a day. As I told you, it is going to take time. Just focus on what you are learning, focus on the movements. Don't be hesitant, and do not let fear of doing something wrong keep you from conquering the movement."

"Yes, sir." Wade turned back to Nick. "Alright. Can you show me one more time?"

"Sure thing, dude. As a matter of fact, why don't you move with me? Just mimic what I do, and we'll run through it a few times until you feel comfortable with it, alright?"

"Alright. Ready."

Connor was faring somewhat better than his friend, but Connor had more motivation than did Wade. The injuries to his face and torso were testament to that, and he was determined that it would not happen again.

He was tired of having to watch his back. Or, more accurately, he was tired of being Zack's punching bag. Learning Jeet Kune Do would help to equalize the situation…or so he hoped.

Sensei Soji was pleased with his young charge's progress. "You are catching on rather quickly, Connor. But do not get a big head. You still have much to learn, and much to practice."

"I understand sensei. But thank you, nonetheless."

The rest of the class was spent on this move: hands up in a proper stance, then moving forward, toe to heel, toe to heel, for ten feet, then turning quickly. By the end of the class Connor and Wade were able to move quite fast.

They took their positions as sensei signaled the end of the lesson. "You have both done well, much better than I had hoped. Continue to practice at home. Tomorrow we will go over it one more time to ensure you have it down, and then on to the next lesson.

"Before you go, listen: you must practice, practice, practice. It should not dominate your life but you must practice every day, away from the dojo. When you wake up, before you go to bed, spare time in the afternoon; anytime you can find to practice, then do so. It will show in your improved performance and you will master techniques more quickly. And now, you are dismissed."

They bowed to their sensei, and then turned to get their things.

As they were changing out of their ghis Mr. Soji stuck his head into the changing room. "Nick, when you get home, take out the trash."

"Yes, sir. See you when you get home, dad."

Mr. Soji shut the door. The boys were done half a minute later and out the door on their way home.

"Tomorrow, guys, we get into punches and blocks."

"Cool!" That got Connor's attention.

"Nothing really fancy or involved, just basic stuff."

"I don't care. At least it's something useful."

Nick stopped and looked at Connor, who stopped as well. "Everything you are learning here is useful. There is nothing that dad is teaching you that does not have a place in the training. He wouldn't waste your time like that."

Connor was embarrassed as he realized how he must have sounded. "Nick, look, I didn't mean it that way, honest."

"Well then how did you mean it?"

Wade stepped in. "I think what he means is that, well, learning movements and stuff is one thing, but it's just a little more exciting, that's all."

"Yeah. That's all I meant. I didn't mean to imply your dad was wasting our time. It's just, after yesterday, I guess I'm a little impatient about learning the good stuff, you know? The punches, the kicks, the blocks."

"Well, that is understandable, I guess. But as dad said, patience is of utmost importance. If you try to rush through it you will be worse off than if you hadn't learned anything. Just be patient. You think I learned all this in a day? Dad started teaching me when I was four years old!"

"Wow, dude. That's amazing." And Wade was amazed. Really.

"Look, I know, O.K.? I'll work on the patience thing."

"Good. 'Cause dad says you're both doing really well."

"Well, I was getting the hang of it tonight, but…I don't know."

"Look, guys. It's a learning curve, O.K.? These are fundamentals. Without the fundamentals you cannot learn the more advanced stuff. Master the fundamentals, worry about the advanced stuff later. Take it one lesson at a time."

"I know. Patience. Working on it."

"Practice tonight, meditate before bedtime, and we'll pick it up again tomorrow. And if you want to practice with me, call me after dinner and we'll go over it. Keen?"

"Got it. Ready for the run home?"

"Ready. Let's hit it."

****

The trio took a circuitous route back to their neighborhood, which pretty much guaranteed that there would be nobody waiting for them along the way. They entered the neighborhood from the opposite direction this time ending up in Nick's driveway.

"Remember, guys, practice tonight. If you need me, I'll be able to help out after dinner and homework."

"Swell. We appreciate it, dude." Wade was a little unsure about his performance thus far, but he was not too concerned. After all, they had just started, and he was sure things would roll right along.

He turned to Connor. "So, dude, we never got a chance to talk today. What did you tell your folks about the battle scars?"

Connor touched his eye, rubbing it slightly. It was still tender and painful to touch.

"I told them I got an accidental hand to the face, causing the black eye. Then I lost my balance and fell on the carpet, causing the carpet burn on my forehead."

"Carpet burn my hind-end!"

"Well, that's what I told them, and that's what you'll tell 'em if they ask. Got it?"

"No worries, dude. Your secret is safe with me."

"So," Nick began, "…what did they say about that?"

"Well, they were concerned, naturally. 'Are you sure it's not too dangerous?' 'Are you up to it?' Blah, blah… I told them it was just an accident and mostly due to me being a clumsy oaf, not to worry, I'll be fine.

"I hate to lie to them, but I really don't want them coming to the school and stirring up the drama that is sure to ensue. So that's my story and I'm sticking to it."

"Alright, then. Well, I gotta get inside. Call me if you need."

"Sure thing. We gotta run as well. Let's go, ding-dong."

“Right behind you, surf-ninja.”

“Surf-ninja? Hey, that sounds pretty cool, dude. Surf-ninja, and his sidekick, the walking wounded!”

“Ha. Ha. Ha. Fun-nee.”

“Yeah, it is. Come on, dude. I can watch you do your algebra.”

“Gee, thanks.”

"Don't mention it," Connor said with a wide grin.

"You don't have to worry about that. I won't"

The two headed off to Connor's house.

****

Wade had stayed over for dinner. He was a sucker for pasta and Mrs. Lundy had made her specialty: chicken-stuffed manicotti. No way he was going to miss out on that.

“Thanks again for feeding me, Mr. and Mrs. Lundy. That was just too awesome for words.”

“Aww, thank you, Wade. You’re so sweet! Hear that, hon? That was just too awesome for words.”

Mr. Lundy conjured up the nicest, most sugary-sweet face he could. “Well, dear, Wade is an incredible suck-up. Wouldn’t you agree, Connor?”

Connor took his cue. “Oh, yeah, man. He’s the king suck-up of all suck-ups. You should see him in school. ‘Can I get anything for you, Ms. Buchannon?’ ‘Do you need any help, Mr. Greevy?’”

“Oh, dude, that is so wrong!”

Mrs. Lundy feigned shock. “Well, Mr. Lundy! Such words!”

Mr. Lundy broke into a fit of laughter, which spread around the room quickly. “Come, now, dear. Wade knows we’re just kidding, right Wade?”

“Absolutely, Mr. L.”

“Well I wasn’t! You're a suck-up!”

“Well you’re a ding-dong!”

They all laughed for a little bit.

“Well, all of that aside," Mr. Lundy looked at Wade with an air of seriousness, "…you think you can look after Connor a little better, Wade? He took a pretty serious hit at practice the other day, didn’t he?”

Connor gave a nervous glance to Wade, who gave him one back. “Well, yes sir. He sure did. I felt bad about it. Don’t know my own strength, I guess.”

Wade immediately smacked himself mentally. Connor never did specify who was supposed to have delivered the blow that gave him the black eye.

They sat silent for a moment. Wade shifted in his seat as he waited for Mr. Lundy to question him further.

“Well,” he began, “…you fellas just be more careful, alright? That’s my only boy, and I need someone to take out the garbage.”

Relief.

Mrs. Lundy chimed in as well. “Yes, you boys please be more careful.”

“Sure thing, Mr. and Mrs. Lundy.” Wade changed the subject, quickly: “Can I help you with the dishes, Mrs. Lundy?”

Mr. Lundy’s face brightened. “See? Connor was right! Suck-up!”

"I told you!"

Wade's face turned crimson. "Aw, come on, guys!"

Mrs. Lundy came to his rescue. "Well, he's just being a gentleman. You could both learn from this fine young man. Of course you can help, Wade. You can help Connor with the dishes."

"I was gonna help, mom. You know that."

"I know, dear. You're both good that way."

Connor and Wade took to clearing the table and began the arduous task of dishwashing and cleaning up the kitchen.

Connor began filling the sink with soapy water. He looked over at Wade, who looked back. "Suck-up."

They both laughed.

****

After they cleaned the kitchen Connor called over to Nick's house. His homework was finished and they had time to spare before it got dark.

"Hey, Nick, are you free? Good. Wade and I will be over in about five. Is that alright? Cool. See you then." He flipped his dad's cell phone shut.

Wade was sitting at the table listening. "Cool. I could use more practice. Let's go."

They shimmied out the back door and headed to Nick's house.

"Wade, that was close. Thanks for not screwing it up."

“No problem. I just kind of winged it. Didn’t go into too much detail ‘cause I wasn’t sure what your story was, but apparently it worked.”

“Well, thanks.”

"And whatever you do, don't show them your leg or your ribs. How are those doing, by the way?"

"Much better. I don't think I broke anything…"

“Hey guys!”

Connor and Wade looked up. It was Nick, who apparently decided to meet them half way.

“’Sup, dude? Ready for us?”

“Sure thing.”

It was a quick jaunt to Nick’s house where they spent the rest of the daylight practicing the moves they had learned earlier that day.

Chapter XXIV: Progression

It had been four months since Connor and Wade began training with Nick and his dad. Mr. Soji was very pleased with their progression, always keeping them together, not allowing one to get ahead of the other.

They had touched on the disciplines of boxing and fencing, as promised, and had also touched on other martial arts like tae-kwon-do, jujitsu, and aikido. They didn't spend a lot of time on those as sensei Soji was focusing on Wing Chun which, he told them, was the purest form of kung-fu, though the other disciplines certainly had many good things to offer to the mix.

Their moves were fluid, they were excellent at retaining balance, and had learned to focus on their attacker while remaining aware of their surroundings. They had also learned how to block a punch, how to deal with an aggressor that was charging them, and had learned some simple, yet effective punching techniques.

They did a lot of sparring with each other. Nick was an excellent sparring partner and a pretty good teacher in his own right, considering he was only thirteen. Then again he had been studying Jeet-Kune-Do since he was four years old. Getting to spar with someone so schooled in the art was very helpful indeed.

After this latest lesson they were sitting on the mat with sensei Soji as they usually did, discussing the lesson, the good points and the bad points, and what to expect the next day.

"Can you both see now how boxing and fencing factor in to the movements and techniques of Jeet Kune Do?"

Connor spoke first. "Yes, sensei. When we began I really didn't see what either one of those disciplines had to do with martial arts, but now it is apparent why you had us study each one before delving into this."

"Yes, sir. I agree with my buddy here. I mean, at first, boxing, yeah, I could see how you would mix it in with martial arts. But fencing? I thought it was crazy, really. But practicing it, studying it, it all makes sense. I can see how it helps us to improve the flow of our movements."

"Remember, all of you. Master Bruce told us that no style is better than any other. You must learn what fits for you. What you have been learning up to now is Wing Chun Kung Fu. As you become more proficient you will begin to experiment with other styles.

"You must not focus on mechanical repetition. When you focus on that, you are focusing on the steps. When you focus on the steps, you lose focus of the task at hand. As you are figuring out what step comes next your assailant is upon you, striking you down.

"What you are learning now is fundamentals. Learn these fundamentals, but do not allow them to define you. Learn what fits for you. Quoting Master Bruce: 'Absorb what is useful, discard what is not. Add what is uniquely your own.'

"You must adapt to the situation. Do not waste time trying to think: 'O.K., how do I counter this punch?' Or, 'How do I counter this kick?' Just do. Do not get lost in thinking up a plan to defeat your opponent. Just defeat him.

"If your opponent slaps you, punch him! If he punches you, kick him! Whatever your opponent lays upon you, you return ten-fold back to him. Make him understand that when he attacks, you will respond with ten times what he gives to you.

"Having said that, remember: we do not go looking for a fight. It is much more honorable to avoid a fight, and if we can avoid it we must. Knowing that, however, you must understand that there are times when a fight is unavoidable. The fight will come looking for you. That is the way it is.

"If someone calls you 'coward' for refusing to fight, do not take the bait. Retain your honor above all else. If, however, your opponent attacks you then, as I said, you may respond, and respond in such a way that he will wish he hadn't attacked you, and that he had allowed you to walk away."

The boys sat in silence, hypnotized by the words of their sensei.

Mr. Soji was about to say something when Connor piped up.

"So, we are supposed to turn away from a fight, because that is an honorable thing to do: to avoid fights when possible."

"Yes, that is correct."

"So, hypothetical: what if I'm faced with a situation like I had before, where I'm walking along, minding my own business, and happen upon some goon terrorizing some little kid, like when I saw Zack jacking up Nick here?"

"In such an instance you must do what you believe to be right, Connor. Did you go looking for Zack to pick a fight?"

"No."

"Did you expect to come across Zack causing harm to someone half his size?"

"No."

"And what did you do when you saw yourself in such a situation?"

"I stopped and stood up for what I thought was right."

"Correct. And that, you must do always."

"I understand. Thank you."

"Now, tomorrow is another day. Let us go."

They all stood up, bowed, and the lesson was over.

Chapter XXV: School's Out

It was the Tuesday before summer break. Two more days to go. Thursday would be the last day, and today was a half-day.

In these last few weeks of school the trio of friends had seen Zack around school from time to time. They avoided any run-ins with him, however.

They took pains to avoid him at school and away from school. They never took the same route home from school twice in a row. If they saw him in the hall at school they turned and went another way; anything to avoid a confrontation.

Most importantly they never, ever went anywhere by themselves. That was just asking for a beating.

Connor and Wade both knew that if Zack caught one of them, or both of them, alone then a fight was sure to ensue. He had already warned Connor who had no doubt Zack was just waiting for another chance to pound his head in again.

Wade didn't feel like getting his tail kicked the first time so he was equally vigilant. However if it did occur that they found themselves in a situation with Zack they felt confident that they could at least somewhat defend themselves, though they were none too keen to try those skills out just yet.

Not that Nick would have had to worry about it, as he so ably proved the last time Zack tangled with him. Even so it was entirely possible that Zack, if faced with an opportunity, may seek to avenge his defeat.

He wasn't convinced that he was really beat, anyway. In the time since their altercation Zack had almost completely convinced himself that he had tripped and fell, that Nick didn't have superior fighting skills after all.

This thought was not lost on Nick, and it was best for all concerned if he just stayed out of his way. For the time being, at least.

Today, however, was the day before the last day of school, and was a half day to boot. The three amigos were meeting up for the trip home. Their plan was to grab some lunch then head to the dojo for an early workout and lesson, leaving more time in the afternoon and evening for free time and perhaps review today's lesson.

Wade and Nick had run into each other in the hallway. When they got to the front Connor was already there waiting for them.

"You guys ready to travel?"

"Yeah, dude. What's for lunch?"

"Whatever we can scare up for ourselves. Mom is great with dinner, but for lunch we're pretty much on our own."

Nick chimed in. "Well, why don't we walk home, and save the run for after lunch?'

"Good idea, dude. Connor?"

"Yeah, I'm down with that. Fine by me."

"Alright, then. We haven't taken the main route home in quite some time. Think we can go that route?"

Nick thought a moment. "Well, it has been a few months. But you never know; Zack may be a lot more patient than we think."

"Well, let's head that way, and we'll hit the trail through the woods at the halfway point. Cool?"

"Alright with me dude."

"Me too. I think that will be fine."

Nick was somewhat more analytical about these things, and with good reason. If he said it was alright then Connor and Wade took it as gospel.

When they arrived at the halfway point they departed from the road and headed into the woods where there was a trail that led to their subdivision. The trail came out in someone's back yard but they knew the family that lived there, the Pearsons, and they had permission to pass through on the way home.

As they entered the wood line Nick took the lead, followed by Wade and then Connor. They had travelled about thirty yards when Nick stopped and turned to his compatriots and held his hand up.

"Everyone stop here for a moment."

Connor stepped up. "What's going on? What's the matter?"

"Yeah, dude, what's the matter?"

"Nothing is wrong. Just stop for a moment and listen."

The trio stood in silence, not moving a muscle as directed.

"Both of you: close your eyes, be very still, and listen."

Connor and Wade were thinking Nick had gone a bit batty, but they did as he asked. The woods were mostly quiet, save for the breeze wafting through the leaves of the trees. There was the sound of something scurrying through the leaves off to one side. A squirrel, Connor thought.

They stood in silence for a couple minutes longer. Finally Wade couldn't take it anymore. "Dude…I'm sure you have a purpose for this. Could you share it with the rest of the crowd?"

Nick opened his eyes and looked at Wade. "What do you hear when you stand still?"

"Uh, duh…the sounds of the forest, dude. Squirrels, wind, birds, leaves. Point?"

"Yeah, Nick. What's the point?"

"Close your eyes again."

Connor and Wade looked at him skeptically.

"Just trust me, guys, O.K.? Have I ever steered you wrong?"

Connor looked over to Wade, shrugged, and closed his eyes. Wade did the same.

"Good. Count to ten. Silently, in your heads, of course. Ready? Begin."

Connor and Wade stood in the middle of the woods, eyes closed, counting to ten in their heads. They felt like idiots, but surely Nick had a reason for it.

It was incredibly quiet: no squirrels darting, no birds flapping, even the breeze had died down somewhat.

They both finished counting at the same time and opened their eyes. They looked at one another, shrugged, and looked around.

"Alright, Nick, what's the big…" And then it dawned on Connor. Nick wasn't there.

"Nick?"

“Dude, he’s over there!” Wade pointed towards Nick who was now standing forty yards away. They were stunned.

“Dude! How’d you do that?” Wade's mouth was agape.

“Yeah, how did you do that? We never heard a thing!”

Nick started walking back towards them. “It takes lots of practice, but with time you will do it too. It is essential for you to learn if we are to be a team.”

Connor folded his arms and shook his head. “That is just too…freakin’…cool.”

“You guys know I stalked you a couple of times before we met, right?”

“Huh?” Connor’s eyes lit up at that. “What do you mean, you stalked us?”

“Yeah. Twice, when you two went fossil hunting. I guess stalking is the wrong word. I was just practicing, that’s all. I was in the woods practicing moving silently when I heard you guys on the tracks. So I followed you. You never heard me or saw me, so I guess it worked.”

“That is wrong on so many levels, dude.”

“You know,” Connor said, “…Wade, remember when we were walking on the tracks that one day and I stopped ‘cause I thought I heard something?”

“Yeah, now that you mention it.”

Nick grinned. “Yep, that was me. I thought I blew it for a moment, but you guys kept walking, so my stealthy moves worked. Well, almost. Also, remember the day you were fighting with Zack and I showed up?”

“Yeah.”

"I had already seen Zack hanging around the neighborhood. So I took my stuff home and came back to where he was through the woods. He never heard me. Then you two showed up. I figured he was waiting for someone."

"Gee. Stalked by a tiny ninja. Whodathunkit?"

"Well, you two are going to learn to move the same way as well. Not today, obviously, but I wanted to give you a heads up. It will be sometime soon. Dad wanted me to teach you guys. Not much silent moving in the dojo, you know."

"Sweet! This is gonna be awesome!" Wade seemed more excited than Connor.

"Alright, lesson over. Let's get home for lunch."

"You lead, little ninja."

"Done. C'mon."

****

Lunch consisted of turkey sandwiches on wheat with sweet tea. Mrs. Lundy was out running errands and Connor's dad was at work. After they cleaned up the kitchen they headed out to get to the dojo for an early lesson.

They decided to take the main route out of the neighborhood as they hadn't utilized that entrance for some time now. They were walking down the street just talking among themselves.

They exited the subdivision and hit the main road, turning left towards the dojo. Nick was the first to see him, and he alerted his companions to his presence.

“Guys, hold up. Look who I see.”

The other two followed Nick’s gaze to the familiar figure coming towards them. It was Zack. He didn’t seem in any particular hurry as he walked nonchalantly, looking as if he didn’t have a care in the world.

The three boys stopped. This was an unanticipated encounter, though not totally unexpected.

“You boys lost?” Zack had that arrogant grin on his face, the look that said ‘I’m bigger than you, I’m better than you, and you better not screw with me.’ It really, really pissed Connor off.

“What are you talking about, freak show? This is our neighborhood. If anyone is lost, it’s you.”

“Oh, hey, little buddy! You healed up real nice! Too bad I’m gonna have to break your face again.”

“Really." Connor began to get angry. "What, you’re gonna do me here, on the street? In front of God and everybody? You gonna take all three of us?”

Nick and Wade stayed put, but remained silent, letting Connor hash it out verbally with their nemesis.

“Nope, not gonna do it now. You just remember what I told you, lunch meat. I’m watching you. All of you. And it may not be today, may not be tomorrow, but one day you’re gonna be alone, without your little girlfriends to protect you. And that day, you will be mine.

“You think the beating I gave you before was bad? I’ve been thinking of new, innovative ways to take your head off, shit stain.”

"Innovative. That's an awful big word for someone as mentally deficient as you. You see that on a billboard on your way over here? You probably don't even know what it means."

"Connor…"

"Shut-up, Wade…" Connor snapped at his best friend.

"Yeah, shut-up, Wade. You're next. And as for you, little China-boy…" Zack looked directly at Nick; "…you got lucky, make no mistake about that. I'll deal with you as well."

"Well, then…why not take me down now?" Nick was calm and spoke almost as if he were ordering lunch at Five Guys Burgers. "Here we are. How hard could it be? This is as good a time as any, no?"

"Three on one? No, I don't think so. I don't like the odds."

"Well then, just the two of us then. You and me."

Zack looked as if he was going to accept the challenge, but thought better of it. "I don't think so. You still have your little friends here to jump in when I start whipping your ass. But don't worry. I'll deal with each of you in my own time."

He looked directly at Connor. "And especially you, panty stain. Count on that." Zack's face hardened into a grim mask of anger and resentment as he stabbed his finger Connor's way. "You boys have a nice day. I'll be seein' ya'." With that he crossed the street and disappeared into the woods.

The three of them stood down, Connor and Wade releasing the tension that had been building in their bodies. Nick wasn't tense at all.

Wade looked at his buddy. "Dude, I don't know in what former life you peed in his Wheaties, but dude has it out for you something fierce."

"You mean he has it out for us, dweeb." Connor was still staring at the patch of woods that Zack had disappeared into.

"Yeah, he has it out for us, but he has a particular animosity for you. By the way, that was funny."

Connor looked at Wade with incredulity. "Funny? What part of that was funny, ding-dong?"

Wade did his best Connor imitation: "'Did you read that on a billboard on your way here?' That was funny. Man, I thought he was gonna jump out of his skin when you said that."

"Oh. Yeah. Well, it seemed like the thing to say at the time."

Nick turned to his friends. "Well, it is obvious he is waiting, and watching. We must be extra vigilant. Especially tomorrow, seeing how it's the end of school and all."

"Yeah. Don't worry. Vigilant we shall be." Connor shook it off. "Come on. Let's get moving."

"Right behind you, oh witty one!" Wade gave a mock salute and a goofy smile, which served to break the tension as they laughed off the encounter.

But they were all concerned. This was not an episode to be taken lightly. Zack had sought them out specifically to deliver a message. What was on his mind? What was he planning? Something was up, that was for sure.

****

Practice that day was spent sparring. Connor and Wade had come a long way from when they first started. Their practice and dedication was paying off and sensei Soji let them know it, even if he didn't outright praise them.

"Keep your hands up, Connor! Never let your guard down! Remember, move as the water! Flow, grace, agility!"

Nick was circling, looking for an opening, but Connor was having none of it. Nick moved in for a shot. Connor blocked and punched back, narrowly missing Nick's chest as he dodged.

Finally Nick saw his chance...he circled once more, waited, and lunged. Connor saw the attack coming. As Nick came forward Connor deftly sidestepped the attack, blocking it almost effortlessly.

As he dodged the attack he countered, sweeping Nick's feet out from under him putting him on his back. In an instant Connor was on top of Nick, hand raised for the coup' de' grace (which he didn't follow through with, of course).

Sensei Soji started clapping his hands. "Excellent, Connor! Excellent! That was an excellent move! Your hard work is paying off."

As Connor got up he offered his hand to Nick, who was flat on his back. Nick took his hand and popped right up.

Connor turned to sensei Soji. "Thank you, sensei."

"Don't get a big head about it. You still have much to learn."

"Yes, sir." He couldn't help but smile as he turned away. He actually took Nick down!

****

The boys decided to walk back home instead of running. They had already run this morning, and besides, they didn't want to wear themselves out with constant exercise. The body needed rest, after all.

Nick tapped Connor on the shoulder. "Hey, you were really on your game today. I mean you were intense. Good move, by the way. I didn't see it coming."

Connor gave an aw-shucks kind of smile. "Heck, I was just in the groove of things, you know? Everything just kind of felt…right. Like everything was falling into place. Almost as if I wasn't controlling my body at all. The moves just came, you know?"

"Yeah, I know. That's good. That means you're becoming more in tune with your body, your mind, and the art of Jeet Kune Do. Keep it up."

Wade piped up. "Yeah, dude. You were like totally into it."

"Well, seeing Zack today helped. I mean, who the hell is he? Coming to our neighborhood, threatening us? Screw him."

"Easy there, tiger. Just keep doing what you're doing. As long as we remain vigilant, we remain together, he can't do anything."

Connor pondered that for a moment. "Well, someone like Zack is eventually going to get tired of waiting. He's got something to prove, and he definitely wants to annihilate me, that's for sure."

“Don’t sweat it, compadre. Some beach time over the weekend will make us forget all of our worries. Who’s up for surfing Friday, first day of summer break?”

Nick’s hand shot up. “Me, for sure! You promised to show me how to surf, remember? I’m gonna hold you to that.”

“Absolutely! I can always use a surf buddy. How about you, ding-dong?”

“Oh, yeah. Got a spare board, don’t ya?”

“Sure do. You guys gotta help me wax them, though.”

“Done. Today?”

“Yes, today. That way they’ll be ready for Friday.”

“Awesome," Nick said. "Tell you what. Let’s take a break from lessons and exercises Friday. I’ll let my dad know that we’re taking the day off. Cool?”

Wade nodded in agreement. “Cool.”

“I’m in as well," Nick added. "I’ll make lunch.”

“Sweeeet.” Wade was all about the surfing, after all.

Chapter XXVI: Set Up

The last day of school for the summer had arrived. What was more: this was the last day of middle school for Connor, Wade, and Nick. Next year they would be in high school. Ninth grade. Low men on the totem pole.

They had heard the horror stories about what happened to freshmen in high school but Connor had figured it was just that: stories. In today's world you didn't get away with much in the way of harassing your fellow classmates. Still, he would be wary and remain vigilant when he got there.

He wasn't going to worry about that today, however. He just wanted to get to school and get the day over with. The run this morning was, as always, invigorating. There would be no lesson today so there was no need to go to the dojo (Mr. Soji said they needed the break and besides, they had earned it). After school he and Nick were going to head over to Wade's house to finish waxing the surf boards for their beach excursion the next day.

After a quick breakfast of toast and OJ he ran out the door and headed to Wade's house. Wade was coming out of the house as he approached. Wade seemed even more ebullient than usual, which was expected on the last day of school before summer break.

"Well, greetings and salutations my most effervescent best friend and next-door neighbor! Ready for the half-a-day that lies before us?"

"Wow. You use big words. What'd you do, fall asleep on a dictionary?"

"Not at all, my man. I'm just happy as heck that school's out for summer as weeks of most excellent surfing stretch out before us. Can't you hear the waves now?" Wade stopped, closed his eyes and put a hand to an ear as he feigned hearing the crashing waves of the surf.

"You're loopy, dude."

They walked up to Nick's front door. As Wade went for the door bell the door the door opened and Nick stepped out onto the porch. "What's up, guys? Ready?"

"As ready as we'll ever be, my little ninja friend."

Connor gave Nick a slight elbow. "He's not really here with us today. Just humor him."

"Oh, right, right. Well, at any rate, just get through today and summer awaits us. We still waxing boards today, Wade?"

"You know it, dude. As soon as school is out, we'll grab lunch and head to the house for a waxing party. And tomorrow, surf's up!"

"Cool. I'm excited to learn how to surf."

"Martial arts I'm getting good at. Surfing, however, is my domain."

"Yeah, Nick. He is good. If you want to learn, he's the guy to teach you."

"Sweet."

They headed up the road on their way to their last day of middle school.

****

The walk to school was uneventful. They talked and carried on as teenage boys do, but they were careful to keep their heads about them, scanning the area and looking for threats. Well, one threat in particular, but he was nowhere to be seen this morning.

Nick headed to his class as Connor and Wade walked to theirs. As they rounded a corner in the hall they caught a glimpse of Zack. He wasn't hard to miss as he stood a full head above most every other student in school.

He hadn't noticed them as they were just another part of the throng of students moving along trying to get to class. Nonetheless they were not taking chances, and turned around to navigate another route to their class.

"Dude, do you think he would try anything in the middle of school, in front of all those people?"

Connor took his seat. "No, I don't think he would. But honestly, we can't be sure, can we? He's not exactly a law-abiding citizen."

"Yeah, good point." Wade took a seat beside Connor. Half the class was out and besides, the teacher really didn't give a rat's rear end about seating arrangements on the last day of school. As long as you kept the talking to a dull roar and didn't make a fool of yourself in front of the class, you were fine.

Wade shifted his desk a little closer to Connor's. "Well, at least we know he's here."

"Yeah. He's here. Yippee."

"Ah, don't sweat it, dude. Three more hours and we're home free. We just have to avoid him."

"Well, it's been working so far, save for yesterday's encounter."

"We'll be fine."

"I'm sure. So, anyway, how long will it take to wax those boards?"

****

The day went by incredibly fast, or so it seemed. The plan was to meet up with Nick at the entrance to the east wing of the school and then head back home for lunch and then the waxing of the surf boards at Wade's house.

Wade had discovered he actually had a third board he had forgotten about so they would each have a board on their surfing excursion, or as Wade started referring to it: "Wade's Surf Clinic for Tragic Non-Surfer Types."

As Connor and Wade made their way through the crowd they kept an eye out for Zack lest he take them by surprise. They didn't think he would be foolish enough to do anything right there in the school, but you never know what someone is willing to do if they're determined. Also, since this was the last day of school, Zack may see this as his last chance to get to them. Would that cause him to lash out? They didn't want to find out.

There was no sign of Zack however, and Nick was waiting for them just inside the doorway that led to the school yard.

"Dude! 'Sup?"

"Not much. Just ready to get home and start enjoying the summer. You guys have any trouble?"

Connor spoke. "No. We saw Zack this morning on our way to class, but we just rerouted and avoided him. No sense taking a chance.

"We kept our eyes open for him on the way here but we didn't see him."

Nick put his hand to his chin as he thought. "Well, it could mean he left early, or you just didn't run into him."

"Or," Connor said, "…he may have just been hanging out this morning with no intention of going to class and left as soon as the bell rang. Who knows?"

"Well, we'll just have to keep our eyes peeled during the trek home. He could be anywhere, and this being the last day of school he may have a plan."

"Alright, well, whatever. Let's just get rolling. We'll take alternate route B, agreed?"

Wade shrugged. "Fine by me."

"Yeah, that'll work." Nick said.

"Good. Let's rock."

They made their way outside blending in with the rest of the multitudes of students streaming away from the building in a rush to get away from the school as quickly as possible, eager to begin their summer break. They had made their way off the school grounds, discussing tomorrow's "Surf Camp" as Wade began to go on about how the martial arts training was actually going to help make him a better surfer.

They had scarcely gotten one hundred yards from the school when they saw the crowd down the street on the opposite side. And the crowd was big.

Connor was the first to notice. "What's going on over there, I wonder?"

Wade and Nick saw it then. They shot a glance at Connor, then to each other.

Nick spoke first. "Well, it probably isn't an end-of-school party, I'm guessing."

Wade spoke next. "Yeah. I'm guessing you're right."

As they drew closer the cacophony of the crowd grew louder. They were animated about something, and that something quickly became apparent.

All three boys said it at the same time: "Zack."

And there he was, in the middle of the crowd, putting some poor sap through the wringer. They couldn't see exactly what was happening or who was getting pummeled, but Connor was going to find out.

"Come on, guys."

Before either of his friends could speak Connor was on his way across the street.

"Ah, crap…here we go. Hey! Wait up!" Wade chased his friend, followed closely by Nick.

The sounds of the crowd grew louder as they approached. Shouts of "…take him!" and "…punch his head in!" could be heard.

Wade was close behind Connor. "Hey, dude? Avoid a fight, honor, all that? Remember?"

Connor looked over his shoulder at Wade. "Hey, dude, do what you think is right? Remember?"

Wade couldn't argue with him on that one so he just shut up. Nick didn't say anything.

They arrived at the scene and Connor immediately began pushing his way through the crowd. He wasn't sure if he was looking to see what was going on or if he really was gunning for a chance to tangle with Zack. No matter.

Wade and Nick were right behind Connor pushing their way through the crowd as well, and ready to back up their friend, crazy or not.

As they breached the front of the crowd a familiar sight greeted them: Zack with some kid in a headlock on the ground. It wasn't a little kid this time; the object of Zack's attention was a pretty good size, but he still seemed to be getting the worst of it.

Wade poked Connor in the ribs. "Dude, this guy can handle himself. He isn't some little kid. Let's bail."

Connor considered this for a moment. "Yeah, you're right. Let's head out."

The moment he said that Zack looked directly at him and stopped. The guy he was struggling with stopped as well.

"Well…lookie who's here. Hello, lunch meat."

The noise from the crowd died down. This was a very unexpected turn of events.

Zack released his "victim," who then took up a position next to him. "Hey, Bobby. Look who's here. It's my buddy panty stain. You know, the one I told you about? The little turd I pounded a few weeks ago? Remember I told you about him?"

Bobby looked over to Connor. "That's him? Man, he's got nads. He's the one been running his mouth off to you?"

Connor didn't get it at first, but it slowly dawned on him what was happening. He had been set up.

Nobody in the crowd got it yet. They were wondering why the fight, their end-of-school entertainment, had been stopped.

"Yup. That's him. Welcome to your end-of-year ass-beating, turd. And look, he brought his little girlfriends with him."

Wade and Nick realized what was happening as well. They took up positions on either side of their friend ready to do what was necessary, if anything became necessary. And it was obvious something was going to be necessary.

Connor took a look around the crowd, then took a step inside the ring, flanked by his friends. "Are you kidding me? You're setting me up? You arranged this…this…spectacle just to set me up and get me to fight?"

"Ain't gonna be no fight, turd blossom. It's gonna be a massacre."

"There you go using words you can't spell again."

"Keep talking smack, dead man. I'm gonna rip your head off and shit down your neck. You've been dogging me for some time, and I ain't gonna have some runt like you make me look stupid."

"Yeah, you're right, doofus. You do a pretty good job of looking stupid all on your own."

"Keep talking. It's just gonna make it worse for you, which is fine with me. Bobby, you keep his little friends away. I'll deal with them later. For now, panty stain here is toast."

Connor shot a glance to Wade, and then over to Nick, who just looked impassive. He then turned his sights back to Zack.

“No, I don’t think so. I didn’t come here to fight. You want to fight someone? Find someone else.” He turned to walk away. “Come on, guys. We’ve got somewhere to be.”

Wade and Nick began to follow Connor's lead. Zack, however, was having none of it.

“What’s the matter? You scared? You chicken? What a pussy! Hey, everybody! Look at the three pussies who won't stand up for themselves! Bunch of cowards!"

Connor didn’t respond as he continued to walk towards the crowd, which had begun to turn a bit rowdy.

“Hey! I don’t think you heard me! You aren’t going anywhere until we’re through here!”

Connor stopped and turned to face Zack. “We are through here. You don’t own me. Who the hell do you think you are? You want to think I’m chicken? Fine. I don’t need to fight you to prove anything.

"Listen to me, and listen carefully: I’m leaving, my friends are leaving, and you ain’t stopping us. So to you I say: piss off and die. Thanks for playing.” He turned to walk away again.

“I don’t think you’re hearing me, runt. Let me put it to you like this: you walk away now, and I’ll follow you.”

Connor stopped in his tracks.

Zack continued, pleased to have his attention. “I’ll harass you. I’ll find you. You won’t get a moment’s peace, ever. You’ll be looking over your shoulder everywhere you go, wondering where I’m gonna be next. You’ll be scared to leave your house. I’ll harass your friends and tell ‘em it’s your fault ‘cause you’re too chicken to fight me.

"So go ahead. Leave now. But you're gonna be sorry. I promise you. And in the end it won't matter, 'cause I'm gonna get to you eventually. So really, you're just postponing 'till later what you can get over with now, and you're putting your friends, what few of them you have, in danger as well. They get hurt, it's on you, shit stain."

As Connor stood there, head down, staring at the ground, hands flexing into fists and then back again, he knew he had no choice.

Wade spoke. "He's bluffing you, man. Screw this guy. Let's go."

Nick spoke next. "Connor, you don't have to do this. He can't force you."

Connor took a deep breath, and then turned back towards Zack. "No. He can't force me. And I don't have to do this...but I am going to do this."

He locked eyes with Zack. "Alright, you piece of crap. You want me? You got me."

A murmur rippled through the crowd. They were going to get their afternoon show after all.

He scanned the crowd briefly, then set his sights back on Zack. "Seeing how you went through all this trouble to arrange this meeting, I guess we'll go ahead and take care of things right here, right now."

Zack's face brightened considerably. "Well, goodie."

He turned to his counterpart. "Bobby, make sure the little squirt's girlfriends stay out of it."

"Sure thing, Zack."

Connor held up his hand and pointed at Bobby. "No, no, no. You don't mess with them. They aren't dishonorable little cheats like you. They aren't going to interfere. This is you and me. You wanted me? You got me. They'll sit on the sidelines, you have my word on that."

Zack snorted. "Your word. What do I give a crap about your word?"

"You wouldn't understand."

"Bobby, keep an eye on them anyway. They so much as twitch, you take them out."

"You got it." Bobby rubbed his hands, gleeful at the chance to show his "bad-ass" side in front of the crowd.

Connor turned to his friends. "Look, no matter what happens, stay out of it. If I'm getting my face pounded, just let it be."

"Dude," Wade looked anxious, "…we're not just gonna stand by and…"

"Yes, you are. I mean it. Don't interfere. If I get my head ripped off, so be it."

Nick clapped a hand on Connor's shoulder. "Remain calm. Don't think, just do. Just like at practice yesterday."

Connor smiled, grabbed his shoulder, and then turned towards the inevitable.

He stepped into the ring, keeping a respectable distance between him and Zack. Meanwhile Wade and Nick melted into the edge of the crowd. It was time.

Chapter XXVII: What Just Happened?

They stood for a moment in silence, Connor sizing up his opponent, Zack just being…Zack.

Connor held his hand up. "Hold on a sec, would you?"

Zack shrugged his shoulders. "For what? Second thoughts?"

"No, just give me a minute, alright? It's obvious you're going to whip my ass anyways, so give me a minute to compose. Condemned man's last request. Is that too much to ask?"

"Fine. Whatever, runt. Make it quick."

Connor took a few steps back as the crowd whispered with anticipation.

"He's scared to death!"

"Little guy gonna get all kinds of beat up!"

Connor didn't pay attention.

After stepping back enough so that Zack couldn't just reach out and tag him Connor turned and faced the crowd, closed his eyes…and began to meditate. He focused on his breathing and emptied his head of anything unnecessary which, he was surprised to find, was not difficult at all this time.

He heard sensei Soji's voice echo through his mind: "…empty your mind…be formless, shapeless, like the water…be water…"

"Hey, nimrod! Let's go! I got places to go, people to see!" Zack bellowed.

Connor didn't respond. "…if your opponent grazes you, punch him…if he punches you, kick him…return to your opponent tenfold what he has given to you…"

"HEY! I said let's GO!" Zack was growing impatient, as was the crowd.

One final deep breath and he opened his eyes. Calm, he turned and faced his nemesis, stepping back into the ring once more. His face was impassive, emotionless, his hands by his sides.

He took no stance, offered no clue as to whether he was even going to defend himself. Connor looked resigned to his fate: a thrashing at the hands of this thug, for no other reason than Zack decreed it was to be.

Zack didn't care if Connor defended himself. Defense or not, the runt was dead meat as far as he was concerned, and if Connor just wanted to stand there and take a beating, that was fine with him. He was going to satisfy his bloodlust…today.

They stood there, looking at one another, neither one making the first move. The crowd began to get impatient.

"Come on!"

"Someone throw a punch!"

"I gotta get home! Hurry up and kill him already!"

Connor didn't flinch. "Your audience is waiting, Zack. What's the hold up? Let's get this party started."

"You're pretty eager to get your ass kicked, aren't you? Fine. Your funeral."

They were about ten feet apart. Zack made the first move and began to close the distance between them. It was his intention to grab Connor by the hair and belt, pick him up and slam him to the ground. His plan, however, didn't quite go as he anticipated.

As Zack approached Connor he brought his hands up. He was about three feet from Connor when he felt the hand on his wrist. Zack began to fall forward though his brain did not register this until he was well on his way to the ground. At about the same time he saw a blur coming towards the left side of his face, and then felt the stinging blow across his cheek bone.

It had happened in a split second: one second he was up, the next second he was on the ground face down, a red welt on the left side of his face between his eye and his ear. He never saw Connor move, didn't see the fist that had connected with his face, never anticipated the move that put him down.

The crowd was shocked into silence. They had never seen anyone take Zack down. It was as if they were witnessing a once-in-a-lifetime event. The silence soon gave way to cheers and yelling.

"Yeah! That's what I'm talking about!"

"Holy crap! Did you see that?"

"No way!"

Connor turned quickly after delivering the blow that took Zack down. He maintained his position, not advancing on Zack. He stood there same as before: emotionless face, hands by his side, looking resigned to his fate as before.

Zack scrambled to get up. He was pissed, as evidenced by the crimson wave of rage that had washed over his face. He wasn't angry at just being hit. He was embarrassed. Embarrassed that this runt, this turd who was half his size had gotten in a lucky punch on him. And he did it in front of a huge crowd.

Zack glanced around the crowd that surrounded them. They were animated, cheering, egging them on to keep fighting.

“Shut up!" Zack bellowed. "All of you shut up, or you’re next!”

This had some effect as the noise died down somewhat, but not completely. Zack then turned his attention back to Connor.

“Lucky shot, turd, but it ain’t gonna happen again!”

Connor said nothing; he just stood there, eyes fixed on Zack.

Zack eased his way closer to Connor, his arms slightly raised in front of him, hands balled into fists. Closer, closer…there! He took a swing at Connor, who easily dodged it. Another swing, another dodge.

Zack stepped back a bit, regrouped, and began to advance once more. He lunged as he took another swing, thinking he would land one on Connor’s face.

Connor saw the lunge and anticipated the punch coming next. He slapped Zack’s fist out of the way with his left hand and instinctively struck with his right, landing a solid blow to Zack’s ribs on his left flank which sent him reeling backwards, though he didn’t fall. The dull ‘THUD’ was heard throughout the crowd which brought another round of cheers and calls from the crowd. Connor wasn’t paying attention to the crowd, but the noise only served to heighten Zack’s rage.

Connor turned again to face his enemy, who was standing near the edge of the crowd, face purple with anger and exhaustion, his face contorted into a grotesque mask of hatred.

Zack was apoplectic, and the sight of Connor standing there impassively, staring at him with cold eyes, only served to push him into a fury.

He brought his right hand up over his head and rushed Connor with the thought of bringing his fist down on top of Connor's head and overpowering him with the sheer weight of his body. He charged with all of the force he could muster, screaming all the way.

It didn't take long to cover the ground between them. He was within striking distance when Connor dropped down. Zack's momentum was too great; he couldn't stop or change course.

The next thing he felt was a floating sensation. The ground disappeared and was replaced by sky, followed quickly by the ground again as he hurtled towards a hard landing.

The wind was knocked out of him as he landed with a loud 'THUD.' He had never had the wind knocked out of him before. It was a scary feeling. He thought he was dying.

A few seconds later his breathing returned. He lay there on the ground, writhing as he struggled to catch his breath. He was breathing heavily. But he wasn't done yet.

Zack struggled to one knee, then to his feet. Connor took a couple steps back, out of Zack's striking distance.

The crowd was hooting and hollering, cheering and cajoling. It was almost deafening for the two combatants. Connor shut it out of his mind, but it was bothering Zack.

This wasn't how it was supposed to be. This little twerp should have folded like a three-dollar lawn chair from Wally World, yet there he was, standing there unscathed, untouched.

Connor's expression never changed. He just stood there as Zack struggled to find his legs.

"I told you I didn't want to fight, but you insisted. You ready to call it quits?"

"Up yours, maggot! I'm not done with you yet!"

Suddenly Bobby darted from the crowd behind Connor. He grabbed Connor from behind, putting him in a bear hug so he couldn't move his arms. At the same time Zack jumped up and advanced towards Connor, fist raised. It looked like he was going to get his hits in after all.

Nick and Wade were momentarily stunned, and hesitated before reacting. Nick yelled at Wade: "You take Bobby, I'll get Zack!"

"Got it!"

Connor had other plans, however. Zack's fist was coming forward, fast, aimed at Connor's head. As he swung Connor lifted his legs off the ground and donkey-kicked Zack in the face causing Zack's head to snap back. He stumbled backwards, falling to the ground, hands covering his nose and mouth.

As soon as he had made contact with Zack's face Connor brought his feet down squarely on top of Bobby's feet as hard as he could. He then leaned forward a bit, and with all the force he could muster he slammed his head backwards into Bobby's face, stunning him.

A split second later he swung downward with his left hand and made contact with Bobby's groin causing his assailant to scream in agony. This last blow caused him to release Connor as he staggered backwards, one hand cupping his groin, the other cupping his now-broken nose. Connor spun and flat-palmed Bobby in the chest causing him to fall down on his rear-end.

Nick and Wade stopped dead in their tracks. Did they just see what they thought they saw?

"Holy crap, dude."

Nick was equally impressed. "Yeah, dude. Holy crap."

Connor did a three-sixty, assessing the scene and scanning for any other threats that may be lurking. Finding none he turned his attention to his rivals.

Bobby was sitting on the ground, crying and sniffling as he covered his broken, bloodied nose with both hands which were overflowing with blood. Zack was lying on the ground next to Bobby, his nose, mouth and chin covered in blood, a result of a split lip and two missing teeth. The welt on his face had begun to turn purple as well.

A hush fell over the crowd. There was no more cheering, no more cajoling, no more carrying on. They were stunned into silence at the sight of Zack…the Mighty Zack, King Bully of the middle school set…laying on the ground in utter, incomprehensible defeat.

Nobody was more shocked than Wade and Nick who were still struggling to digest what they had just witnessed. They had no idea he had it in him. He defeated not just one, but two assailants at once!

Connor walked over to Zack, who was still lying on the ground moaning in pain, hands covering his mouth, blood running down his chin and neck, his shirt stained red. Zack's eyes locked on Connor's as he kneeled down beside him.

Wade and Nick exchanged puzzled glances. "Dude, what is he doing?"

Nick shrugged his shoulders. "I don't know, but be ready, just in case."

"Right."

Connor looked at Bobby. "Don't you ever bother me or my friends again. Got it?"

Bobby, tears streaming down his cheeks, blood pouring out from under his hands, could only nod. His sobbing prevented him from speaking.

"You really should find better friends."

Bobby nodded again.

Connor then turned to Zack. He grabbed Zack by the hair, lifted his head off the ground, and got nose-to-nose with him. "Now, listen, and listen carefully. Are you listening?"

Zack nodded, eyes wide with uncertainty at what Connor might do to him next.

"Good. Quit bothering me. Quit bothering my friends. Quit bothering my classmates. I'm not taking any more crap off you, and neither are my friends. Leave us alone.

"If you persist in harassing us you will regret it. I will beat you mercilessly. You think today was a beating? Let me catch you harassing my buds again. I will beat you so bad your parents will need dental records to identify you…that is, if they can find your teeth. Do you understand me?"

Zack nodded rapidly, acknowledging that he did, indeed, understand.

"Good."

He dropped Zack's head on the ground, generating a small 'thud' as it made contact with the ground.

"We're done here."

Zack said nothing.

Connor got up, brushed the dirt off his knees, and began walking towards his friends. As he did so someone in the crowd began to clap, followed by a couple more people, then more, until finally the whole crowd was applauding.

Connor did not acknowledge them as he walked up to his friends. "Come on, guys. Let's get home. We got some surfboards to wax."

His buddies said nothing as they followed him through the crowd that was still applauding. They were still too stunned at the scene that had just unfolded before them.

As they broke through the throng the crowd began to disperse, leaving Zack and his accomplice writhing on the ground, moaning in pain. Connor could hear their sobbing as he walked away. He didn't look back.

The walk home was quiet and uneventful. Summer break had begun.

Chapter XXVIII: What Comes Next

Friday, the first official day of summer break was upon them. With newly waxed boards the three boys made it to the beach early to catch the incoming tide. Connor had brought the food that would get them through the day and they all had a little pocket change for snacks later on.

Wade was in his element. Today it was his turn to be the teacher as he laid some pointers on his buddies about surfing.

They were sitting on their blanket, virtually alone on the beach save for a couple out walking their black lab and a trio of bike riders making their way along the surf line.

It was a gorgeous day. A stiff wind was coming in off the ocean, the waves were swelling, and the smell of the salt air served to remind all just how great life is.

"Dudes! So, like, are we ready for high school, ya' think?"

Nick spoke first. "Well, judging by Connor's performance yesterday…yes, I do believe we are."

Connor gave an "aw-shucks" smile and looked down, embarrassed by the attention. "Come on, guys. It's over. Let's just forget it, alright?"

"Dude! How are we supposed to forget that? That was awesome! I mean, not awesome that it happened, but, I mean, you took out two guys at once! One of whom, may I remind you, has been tormenting you, me, and countless others for months at school. No, there will be no forgetting that one, my friend."

"Whatever."

Nick spoke next. "Well, Wade's right. Fighting is nothing to be proud of, but like I said: sometimes you have no other option. You gave him the opportunity to forget it, but he made it impossible for you to *not* engage in a fight. That's on him, not you."

"I suppose."

"Well, at any rate, Monday we get back into the swing of things. There is a lot more to learn, always."

"So, are we gonna be a team, or what?" Connor asked. "And if we are, what is our purpose gonna be?"

Nick pondered this for a moment. "Well, as dad told us, we are not to go looking for fights, nor do we go looking for revenge."

"I don't want to pick fights, Nick. I want to be able to keep people like Zack from preying on people like us. I want to move undetected. I want to be able to stop things like Zack from happening to others. I want…"

"Hold on! Hold on! Don't go getting all vigilante on me, big guy!"

Connor took a deep breath.

Wade piped up. "I think what our most excellent friend is trying to say, ninja master, is not that we should be vigilantes, but we should be guardians of the realm, so to speak."

"Yeah, that's all. Think about it: there isn't anyone to come to the aid of those too weak to defend themselves, is there? They're easy picking for people like Zack. We could equalize that."

Nick thought for a moment. “So, you want to form, like, a team of ninjas?”

“Not ninjas, dude. Gosh, that sounds so corny. A team, yes. Utilizing ninja-like techniques? Yes. Not to go looking for fights, but to keep them from happening.”

“I think I see what you are saying. O.K. I’m in. Wade?”

“Oh, yea, dudes. I’m in. I need to improve my skills and all, but, yeah. I’m in.”

“Alright, then. It’s settled. We have a whole summer with which to learn new skills and improve those we already have. I’ll talk to dad about it, too. We need to get his approval for it for sure.

"And nobody must know about it! We must remain unknown.”

“Yeah,” Connor agreed, “…for sure.”

Wade was excited about it. “Cool! I can’t wait! But enough of that for now. We can discuss the particulars later. Who’s ready to surf?”

“Sweeeeet! Let’s boogie!”

They grabbed their boards and headed for the water. Summer had begun in earnest.

-fini-

CPSIA information can be obtained at www.ICGtesting.com
Printed in the USA
BVOW081433070113

310000BV00016B/759/P

9 781456 423315